Allison and I talked right round every subject we started. I was watching her, watching her cross and re-cross her legs, watching her flexing the muscle of her thigh rhythmically. I watched her lower her head so some of her thick, shiny hair fell over her eyes.

'Do I look prettier this way?' I expect she was thinking.

I had purposely sat her down on a chair a long way from mine so I could take her in. She was going to be good in bed. I would see to that. . . .

THE SECRET WEB

Jane Ann Roberts

A STAR BOOK

published by
the Paperback Division of
W. H. Allen & Co. PLC

A Star Book
Published in 1986
by the Paperback Division of
W. H. Allen & Co. Plc
44 Hill Street, London W1X 8LB

Printed in Great Britain by
Anchor Brendan Ltd, Tiptree, Essex

ISBN 0 352 31852 X

Author's Note

The characters and incidents in this story are entirely fictitious and bear no resemblance to any living person or actual events.

J.A.R.

'Down the swift Hebrus to the Lesbian shore . . .'

John Milton

❖ 1 ❖

Chapter 1

When women start to be awfully nice to me I always know what they want. And I am not often wrong.

What surprised me about this one was how young she was. She was pretty, fair-haired and only just 18. Allison's mother was my best hated rival and so I was, secretly, rather pleased.

As soon as I was quite sure, and Allison had fetched and carried for me to her heart's content, I asked her if she would like to spend the night at my home. She was delighted and her large, blue eyes filled with tears as she said, 'Oh that would be so nice. And it will break the long journey for me.' She lived about 100 miles further on.

I looked at her slim, small-breasted figure and mentally undressed her. She was a few inches taller than me but that would not count in bed. And that was where she was going to end up.

When I got her home, I made her wait for it. My devoted husband, with whom I lived in perfect harmony, had gone to bed at 10 p.m., as he usually did, and I sat and talked to Allison, never taking my eyes from hers.

She had gone through all the routine, fluffed up my cushion before I sat down. Her flattery was quite transparent:

'Is there anything I can do to help you?'

'I wish I was smooth and elegant like you.'

'You were kind to ask me to stay.'

But how did she know I was butch? I do not look butch. Someone must have told her, some cat on the prowl. Women are like that. That is why I do not greatly like them. I prefer men, except for one thing. And the one thing that I can not do without is women. It is, I have often thought, an extraordinary paradox.

We talked right round every subject we started. I was watching her, watching her cross and re-cross her legs, watching her flexing the muscle of her thigh rhythmically. I watched her lower her head so some of her thick, shiny hair fell over her eyes.

'Do I look prettier this way?' I expect she was thinking.

I had purposely sat her down on a chair a long way from mine so I could take her in. She was going to be good in bed. I would see to that. Even if bed were only to be a sofa in the first instance.

We started to talk about clothes. About summer clothes, winter clothes, night clothes and then about bras. It was typical woman's chat, not normally my scene.

I asked her if her mother would mind if I bought

her some underclothes for Christmas. And she blushed.

On the subject of bras, I said I had a narrow back and a 38-inch bust, and could never get the right sized cup. She offered to shop round for me in London.

'I am sure I can find what you need if I go round enough shops. I'd gladly do it for you.'

I said that would be nice and I slowly unbuttoned my blouse and pulled up my bra to show her my full, naked breasts.

'Let me look at your bra,' I said.

'I haven't got one on,' she replied.

'That's all the better,' I said. 'Come here.'

I slipped my hand inside her dress and cupped her naked breast, which just fitted my hand. Then I kissed her. It was not a sisterly kiss. I put my tongue straight in her mouth and pulled her to me demandingly.

Then I deliberately let a note of mock harshness enter my voice:

'Allison, when I kiss you, open your mouth. I am used to getting my own way.'

I pulled her down in the chair, running my fingers through her soft, fair hair to remove the clip she wore. I like a girl to have her hair loose when I make love to her.

After a while I took her over to the sofa and moved my body suggestively against hers.

I made her undress herself. There is something rather sensuous about a girl removing her clothes at the order of another woman. I shook my things off, rather than removed them, and prised her legs open with my knee. Then I touched her. She was all ready for me and had been for sometime, by the feel of it.

Now it was my turn to feel impatient. I opened her slim, smooth thighs and buried my head between them. She caught my brown hair in her hands as if to hold me off, but nothing could stop me. I put my mouth to her wide open vagina, slipped my tongue inside her and drank from her as if from a well.

Allison surrendered and went limp in my hands. Then I took what I wanted.

I wondered what her mother would say if she knew. I did not like her mother, but I was enjoying her daughter.

Allison climaxed all too soon. She made so much noise I thought she would wake the house up, but I made no attempt to shush her. I like the sound of a girl's orgasm and the more uncontrolled the better. I wished her mother could have heard. The thought excited me.

Then I moved up on her now limp body and kissed her mouth.

'Now she'll know what she tastes like,' I thought maliciously, putting my tongue inside.

Poor Allison, but she had asked for it and she had got it. She was just a young girl learning about life from an older woman. My large full breasts covered hers and I had my thighs firmly between her wide open legs.

It was then that she discovered that a woman's clitoris, or mine anyway, will reach those parts she thought only a man could master. She climaxed again and this time I did too.

I did not dry her this time. I made her close her legs and go to sleep in my arms with her sex covered with wetness – my wetness. I held her firmly in my arms and grasping her hair, bunched up, in my hand, putting her mouth to my breast.

When we woke, some two hours later, it was to find the nipple had been sucked to twice its length. And in her sleep too.

Gathering up her clothes, I took her upstairs, and got into bed with her. I put her mouth to my other breast this time, and my hand between her legs. She was wide and open again and when I tasted my fingers I found they just tasted of me. I have often noticed that I can dominate the sexual scent of another woman just by having an orgasm over her vagina. And, with little 18-year-old Allison, I had had a longer, deeper climax than I can ever remember. It was partly she was so young and pretty, and partly because I disliked her mother so. Being sexually intimate with her young daughter was a sort of personal revenge. I only wish I could have let her know. Perhaps she would find out one day. I hoped she would, I thought, wickedly.

But Allison was purring. Oh, she loved me, didn't she? Would I do it again? I did, twice more, before we both slipped into the depths of sleep, naked and entwined together, her face buried in my hair. To hell with her mother. Allison was mine.

At breakfast my husband read the paper, oblivious

to Allison's presence. The girl had obviously had a rough night, judging by the state of her once smooth and shining hair. I must wash it for her before she goes home, I thought.

Actually my husband knew exactly what had happened. He gets a kick out of it, but I will never let him join in. I always promise to tell him everything and he has to be content with that. I can share a girl with another woman, perhaps because that is what happened to me when I was a not very reluctant victim in my youth, but never with a man.

'Can I come and stay again?'

'Yes, of course you can,' I replied.

I thought, but did not say, 'When you next come it is going to be a threesome and I am going to give you to my friend, Margaret.'

I kissed her on the top of her head, very chastely, and took her off to wash her hair, having another orgasm over her as I did it. I felt it coming just in time and, grasping her wet, soapy locks in one hand to keep her still, knelt over her face. I rubbed my vagina, hot and sticky, over her face and lips and climaxed all over her. I held her still in that position for a minute or two, savouring the essence of the waves of sexual pleasure the assault had given me. I had been so rough with her that she started to cry, which in the brief enjoyment of the experience, I ignored. I had probably frightened her with the intensity of my orgasm and the tightness of my grip in her wet hair.

I soon cheered her up. Once she had bathed and had her hair re-washed, she was as affectionate as ever. Shocked a little, I suddenly realised that it was her mother that had made me do it. But this was only the beginning. I was going to do a lot more to eager little Allison before I was finished with her. And she would love it. So far nothing I had done had slaked the fires within me or completely satisfied her. That was to come.

I kissed her on the mouth. 'I'll come again if you'll ask me,' she said.

'All right, I ask you,' I said. 'Be here the same time, same day, next week. And don't tell your family where you are going.'

'I'll tell them later,' I thought, 'that might even be the best part.'

I kissed her again, our wet, nude bodies glued together, my hair nearly as wet as hers.

'And no holds barred next time,' I said, just to excite her teenage curiosity. 'You have been warned!'

'I don't mind what you do, as long as you enjoy it, I will too. I don't even mind what you did then,' she hesitated, 'after all, it is only what a lioness does after it has caught its prey, to mark it as hers. I'm your prey I suppose!'

'Well you were not very hard to catch,' I said, 'come on, let's dry your hair.'

I took her into the bedroom and locked the door. When I had dried her hair and combed it out, loose and shining like a golden curtain, I put her on the bed and made love to her yet again. This time I was very gentle and she clung to me as she climaxed. I had the whole of her right breast in my mouth at the time and I bit gently as she finished, which brought her on again to a double orgasm. Once again I made her lie there, wet and warm, with her legs closed. As we were not so tired this time, we lay together and talked. I put her hand down between her legs, then made her taste her fingers. 'Do that tonight before you go to sleep,' I said 'and you'll dream of me.' 'I taste like you,' she said 'and that's nice.' Then she said something startling: 'May I call you Jane?' I suddenly realized she had never used my Christian name before, I had just been Mrs Roberts, her mother's friend, up till now.

'In bed, yes,' I retorted, 'but not otherwise.' Then I kissed her deeply, my tongue in her mouth. 'And never forget you are my prey.' She giggled. She was only a schoolgirl really, or a college girl at best.

As soon as her car had gone down the drive for home, I rang Margaret and fixed a date for lunch.

Actually, we never had lunch at these sessions, just a few gin and tonics and straight to bed. Her husband, after three years, had never even guessed at our relationship. He was an unimaginative man anyway. According to Margaret, he made love like an animal, roughly, before she was ready, merely to satisfy himself.

I took Margaret upstairs about half an hour and four gins after arrival. We both undressed before we even kissed, we always do, and then I slid in between the sheets of her double bed, taking the place of her husband Paul.

As I fingered her vagina with my left hand I stroked back her light brown hair from her forehead. She wore her hair straight, shoulder length and in a fringe. Then I told her about Allison and what I wanted her to do.

Margaret was 32, and very feminine. Under expert control she could, however, make a good job of being 'butch'. And I was the expert. As I expected, she agreed at once with my demand. She was a little jealous I could see, and this was one way of dealing with them both.

'I shall make love to Allison with you lying beside us close, very close. And just before she climaxes I shall make her have it with you.'

I went down on Margaret. Her genitals were wide open like the figure O, and there were two bruises on the inside of her thighs made, no doubt, by Paul's last effort.

She had an orgasm in my mouth. The only time she ever climaxed, it was with me. I suppose Paul thought she was frigid, but I could have told him differently. I was fond of Margaret, she was the only lesbian girlfriend I had ever really been fond of. I dried her gently with my mouth. I was always gentle with Margaret but I said to myself, 'I won't be when I have her in bed with Allison. After I have let her have the girl, I will take her and make love to her as I have never done before, demandingly and insistently. Just for the benefit of Allison, who will be lying in the same bed, neglected and watching. Then I'll have her too.' I squirmed at the prospect.

The thought left a warm feeling at the base of my tummy. I seized Margaret's leg between my thighs and worked myself off. Margaret did her best to help, running her fingers through my hair and inserting her tongue in my mouth. That was why I liked her, I supposed, she was always co-operative and always ready for it.

And tonight Paul would wonder why she was especially uninteresting!

'Promise me you will refuse Paul tonight,' I said.

'He won't let me refuse. If I do, he just puts it in with my arm twisted behind my back. Matter of fact, he seems to enjoy it better that way. He's very big and he hurts me with his penis when he gets too excited. It seems to get even bigger. But I will refuse him if you want me too. He'll take me just the same though.'

'Yes, refuse him,' I replied. 'And if he hurts you, I'll make up for it next time. We'll have our own back on him.'

'He'll hurt me all right,' said Margaret. 'The trouble is he will love every minute of it. I usually give in straight away because of that.'

'Well, fight to the last this time,' I told her, 'and when he hurts you we'll secretly hurt him back, here in this bed – or mine – at the very first opportunity.'

I had a fair idea that she liked being hurt, mentally, because whenever he hurt her, she betrayed him with the greatest enthusiasm in my arms the very next time. There was method in my madness. I was fond of Margaret, but even then it did not worry me in the least that she should be hurt to increase my personal pleasure.

'When you next see me,' said Margaret, 'those bruises on the insides of my thighs will be fresh.

He even opens my legs after he has forced me, and admires his handiwork. He once said he likes to see two black bruises and his sperm running out of my vagina.'

The thought was exciting her I noticed. She was a bit of a masochist. I went down on her again and she climaxed almost at once.

'I wasn't thinking of him,' she told me apologetically, 'I was thinking of what you are going to do to me when he has forced me.'

'Whatever he does I will make it up to you. Just you do as you are told by me, and refuse him. I like to think of you being manipulated by me, as if by remote control. It shows you love me.'

'I'll show you,' said Margaret, 'I really will.'

'And I will love you, darling, as you have never been loved before.' I did not often use the word 'darling' to a woman, only to Margaret, and only when she did just what I wanted.

I felt relaxed and happy as I drove back. It was all going to work out as I wanted it.

But there is a problem in organizing a threesome with women, you have got to get three charts and spread them on the floor and then see how the dates coincide. Finally, I set a date. My husband was going to London and the house would be free. The telephone solved the rest of the problem. All that was left was the stage management on the day. And that, too, was my job and, at this I was an expert.

It would only be the beginning. I was resolved to keep Allison as my personal side-kick, but make

her do what I wanted as a reward. And what I
wanted in the first instance was for her to submit
herself to Margaret and then, perhaps – and the
thought entranced me – with other women. I am
not very nice, I concluded, but they keep on coming
back for more – so does it matter? Women, and as
a woman I should know, have a strange fascination
with self-destruction. On the other hand I thought,
it is only in the mind, no girl has ever really been
harmed by what I do to them.

The next day I was not so sure. Margaret rang me
tearfully at nine o'clock. Would I go and see her?
I did, at once.

She was still in bed. There was a bruise on her
cheek and she had been crying. I got some cold
water and a sponge and bathed her face. Then I
slipped off my clothes and slid into bed with her.

'Did you succeed in refusing him?' I demanded.

'No' she said. 'Nearly, but not quite. I told you
I couldn't. He always makes me.'

'Well, what happened?'

'I wouldn't let him, as you said. I *wouldn't*, but
he did it just the same. And he beat me. He twisted
my arm too.'

'He's a beast,' I replied.

I felt her bottom and sure enough there were the
marks. Not heavy ones, but he'd beaten her all
right. I kissed her and she came to me like one
magnet to another, clinging to me for comfort.

And I gave her comfort. Heavy maternal
comfort, laced with sex. And she lapped it up.

The bruises were there. He had forced her. The thought excited me. It was as if I had done it.

'I've never known his penis so large, and he rammed it in despite my struggles, and he came after just a few thrusts.'

She smelt of male sex. Sex, beer and tobacco. Her hair was sticky with saliva or something.

I pulled her out of bed and bathed her. When she was clean and washed, and I had dried her pretty, light brown hair, I put her back into bed and made love to her. She was so ready for sex, female sex, that I was glad I had encouraged her to oppose her drunken husband, for that is what he had been, drunk. Not so drunk he could not do it, just drunk enough to crush the summer flower of his beautiful wife, to haul her into the bed with brute force, and then to rape her roughly. And it was my fault. It was my fault, but I reaped the benefit. She was so ready for my mouth that when I opened her legs to lick her out, I could almost have fallen inside.

I gazed hungrily beyond the black bruises on her inner thighs at the lips of her vulva, puffy because they too had been stretched and battered. I bent to caress her and as I licked, I tasted his sperm, male and salty. He had ejaculated in his wife, whether she wanted it or not. And the protesting wife, grateful for the softness of my warm tongue, climaxed as I had never known her do so before. With every movement of her hips towards my mouth she betrayed him – betrayed him and hated him. All this was heaven for me. We made love together, and she wept in my arms as I climaxed too. Men like Paul do not know what they are doing when they think they can batter their wives into liking sex. The only thing is, it is women like me, waiting in the wings, who gain the benefit, so why should I grumble?

After that, Margaret was even more ready to do what I wanted her to do with Allison. There would be no force, just persuasion; no roughness, no brutality, just silky softness and female sex. Sex and seduction of the young are wrong I suppose, but the way I do it, except for side effects, like the rape of Margaret, no one ever suffers anything worse than an orgasm. A lesbian orgasm from the lips of a dominant female, never did any girl any harm. Heavens, I was first seduced by a girl when I was 16 and I loved it. The same thing cannot be said of male domination.

But back to the work in hand. Margaret was to come and stay the night and so was Allison. Neither husband or mother suspected anything. The plans were laid, but would they work? I had to get rid of my husband John somehow. He was too curious. He would not interfere but he might get in the way. If I let him he would join in, but that would spoil it. Allison was going to be in the hands of women only, with the front door locked and all night for us to relax in – if relaxation is the word.

I wanted no interference, no interruption, nothing but lesbian sex from cocktail time till dawn, with Allison and Margaret naked in bed and under my control. That was what I wanted and that is what I intended to have. My mouth was watering. I could taste Allison's vagina already. When she volunteered to be my girl I do not think she really knew what was in store for her. When I get my talons into a girl who excites me, she never gets away until I am done and finished with her. When I say, done and finished, that simply means 'until all passion fades,' as it usually does in lesbian affairs. They start with the brilliance of a magnesium flare and flicker out after a few months or, at the best, a few years. That had been my experience to date.

But, with Margaret, the flare was still quite bright, until one saw it against the brilliant light of Allison and her passion for me. Quite frankly, although I did not return her passion with quite the same depth of sincerity, she fascinated me. That was why I was going to make her submit herself to Margaret, to be unfaithful to me against all her instincts and inclinations. Lesbian love is much more twisted than heterosexual love – devious, perhaps, is a better word. So much more of it is in the mind. Poor Allison suspected nothing, she just adored me with a single-minded passion, which precluded all reason. She would do anything I wanted, she had said, anything. And I was going to keep her to her word. Allison was about to encounter a phenomenon known to sexual science as the theme of the dominant female. I was the dominant female and Margaret and Allison the subordinate ones, I felt my pulse quicken.

We all met up at an agricultural show, Margaret and Allison knew each other by sight already. Altogether we spent a pleasant day looking at ponies and dressage trials.

And piling into our cars we sped homewards. As soon as we got in I said:

'Let's all go off and have baths, the water's hot, and then change into something really comfy for drinks. I am going to wear my pyjamas.'

We had two bathrooms, so I went off to one with Allison, to her delight, and left Margaret to the other.

As soon as I had locked the door I took Allison in my arms for a long kiss and undressed her and put her in the bath with the mixer tap on warm. I tied her fair hair up so it would not get wet. I wanted her to look her best this evening. I had plans for her.

Allison was thrilled. I expect she thought there would be a few drinks and then to bed in our respective rooms with me tiptoeing down the corridor to hers, after a decent interval. She was pleased my husband had gone to town. Perhaps I would stay with her all night, with no husband to go back to.

I undressed slowly and stood nude before her, my great, dark bush of pubic hair – I have a lot of hair there – standing out at the base of my flat stomach, a few inches from Allison's mouth. My heavy, well-supported breasts both showed signs of being sucked by someone fairly recently. I looked down at Allison and, taking her face between my hands, pressed it to my Mound of Venus. It had been a hot day and we had walked miles and I wanted the girl to smell the full, strong scent of a grown woman on heat, because that is what I was. I stepped into the bath and, putting my legs either side of her face, made her wash me clean with her tongue.

Then I got into the bath with her. My full, mature female form and her tall, slim, almost adolescent figure forming distinctive contrasts. I lent forward, covering her small, firm breasts with mine, I noticed that they were at least four times their size. I kissed her again, just to taste myself on her lips.

'I want you to be very nice to Margaret tonight. Whatever advances she makes to you, you are to let her have her way.'

'What!' said Allison. 'Be unfaithful to you, never. I couldn't.'

'You'd better,' I said, 'or I am finished with you. You must always do what I tell you.'

As far as I was concerned, that concluded the conversation. I bathed the girl, dried her on a large white towel and then dressed her in her pink school-girl nightie and dressing gown. I brushed out her hair and scented both her hair and her body, especially in the vital areas. She looked sweet. Sweet and very young.

Then I slicked back my dark hair and pinned it up and put on my black pyjama apres-ski outfit including, believe it or not, rubber spurs. I looked quite dashing. And very butch. That was the intention of course. I can look very feminine if I try. And I usually do try. Allison had never seen me in this mood. Or looking like this. I think it worried her a little.

I led her into our bedroom, holding her by the hand, to find Margaret with a glass of gin and tonic, reclining at her ease and wearing a blue nightie, very low cut. I thought she looked lovely with her head on the pillow of our king-sized bed. I poured a drink for Allison and drew the heavy curtains and turned down the lights. Then I took Allison by the hand and cuddled up to her, next to Margaret. Very deliberately I put my hand inside her nightdress and fondled her breasts. Allison looked round, surprised I suppose, and I kissed her on the mouth. I slipped the shoulder of her dressing gown off and the strap of her nightie to expose her breast to Margaret's view. I pushed her down on the bed and pulled Margaret close beside her, so her lips touched the girl's cheek, while my lips were on her mouth.

My left hand pulled up her dress and my fingers started to caress her leg and then her vagina, which was wet and open already. Pulling off my pyjama trousers I slid over and mounted her. There was a faint protest from Allison so I took Margaret's hand and introduced it between us pushing her fingers inside the girl's genitals. Then, taking Margaret's head, I guided it over Allison face and let them kiss.

I coaxed Allison to behave. I told her to return Margaret's kiss. Gently I supervised them both. I removed Margaret's nightdress myself and then pulled Allison's down so they were both naked. I pulled Margaret on to the girl and eased Allison's legs wide open to allow for unrestricted access. Then I put my arms round them both and told

Allison to give Margaret everything she wanted. It
worked like a charm. After a while I pushed
Margaret down on Allison, whose mouth I now
took over myself.

'Don't hold anything back,' I said, 'let Margaret
do what she wants.'

Every time I sensed Allison was about to climax
I thrust my head in Margaret's hair and pulled her
off. I teased poor Allison so much she was nearly
in tears, as she strained upwards.

'All right,' I said, 'put your hands in Margaret's
hair and hold her to you.'

She had no sooner done so than she climaxed. I
removed my mouth from hers so that the noise she
made was not muffled.

Then I took Margaret in my arms and to Allison's jealous chagrin, made love to her, being
super-affectionate. Allison lay neglected beside us,
I pulled her close in so that she felt and heard the
lot. I enjoyed making her jealous and, towards the
end, guided her mouth to Margaret's breast.

When I went to sleep it was Margaret that I
cuddled. Allison was made to sleep in the curl of
Margaret's body.

'You are Margaret's girl for tonight,' I ordered,
'so do everything she tells you.'

Quietly I switched the light out and three naked
female bodies cuddled up under silk sheets and in
each other's arms. For Allison this was going to be
the first of many occasions when I would simply
give her away – just for kicks. It amused me and
it both hurt and excited her. For the rest of the
night it was Margaret making love to Allison and

me to Margaret. I refused to touch the girl until the morning when, for the first time, I took Allison in front of Margaret and went all the way. I left nothing to the imagination and Margaret watched it all, propped up on her elbow. For a successful threesome it really took a lot of beating and this was by no means my first.

It was, however, the first time for Allison, who had given herself to both of us with almost equal passion.

'I feel sort of cheap,' she muttered, looking somewhat crestfallen.

'Well, you are a bit shop-soiled I suppose,' I comforted her, 'but we love you. And you'll soon get used to it. Incidentally, now I am in charge of you I want you to let your hair grow longer.'

'Mummy doesn't like it long.'

'What your mother wants is no concern of mine. You do as you are told by me from now onwards.'

'All right,' said Allison 'as long as you'll love me.'

'I told you I loved you,' I said, 'and for that you can prove you love *me* – with Margaret, now.'

Once again I made her submit while I watched and supervised. Margaret was quite good, seeing she was really femme and wanting it herself. What I can make women do, I thought!

Margaret had her hands twined in Allison's soft, golden hair, dragging her head back over the pillow. Her mouth was working at the girl's breast, her clitoris, nearly as pronounced as mine, I noticed, burrowing into the girl's pubic hair to touch hers in mutual pleasure. I stroked Margaret's light brown hair to encourage her. As I did so, she bit into Allison's breast which caused a cry of pain which merged into a climax. I had often done that to Margaret. She was returning it, with interest, to a younger woman.

We had nothing to do that morning, so we all went to sleep again. This time we put Allison between us, on her back, and each of us put one leg over hers, each had an arm round her, each had her lips to her cheek. I had my fingers against her vagina. Margaret cupped one breast in her hand. Both of us kissed her on the mouth before, with a sigh, we drifted off to sleep.

Allison complained she dreamed of sex all the time she was asleep. Well, she would, on her back, would she not?

After that we dressed and went down to sit in the sun in the garden. For once I was completely relaxed and when Allison came and sat by my feet, I made her go and sit by Margaret.

'Next week, Allison, on Thursday morning you are to go down to Margaret's home and submit yourself to her. For this Margaret has given me her husband's cheque for £20. He thinks he is buying scent for his wife, actually he is buying sex for his wife.'

I ran a scent agency for one of the national companies as a sideline.

It amused me making Margaret be butch, when she was really femme, and it gave me a kick turning Allison into a lesbian prostitute.

'And I shall have a report from Margaret as to how you were. So you had better be affectionate and sexy. And tonight you can sleep alone with me.'

Before Margaret left I made her take Allison inside and make love to her yet again, while I sat, with feigned indifference, in the garden. When they came out, I said to Margaret:

'That's the last lay you get free. You have to pay from now onwards. Or Paul has to pay', I said mischievously. 'Was she all right?'

'She had another orgasm with me, if that's what you mean', smiled Margaret, 'she's really quite hot stuff for a well educated young lady.'

But, in reality, we were only play acting. I supplied Margaret with her £20-worth of scent, so her husband was not being cheated, and Allison was not being prostituted at all. But she thought she was and Margaret told me she was three times as sexy alone with her as she had been the first time.

The truth of the matter is some girls and women like being prostituted by the women they love. This is why so many lesbians are successful call girls. I knew that this was the case when they went with men, but that the same applied when they were made to do it with other women was news to me.

I had to tell little Allison that we were only teasing her and that Margaret would get her scent just the same. The only thing was that it might spoil the whole set up. Now that she had got used to the idea Allison was pleased to do this for me.

'I try to be sexy with her for your sake,' she explained. 'It doesn't make you jealous does it?'

I must tell her one day, just to clear my

conscience. Meanwhile I reward her with kisses and the occasional expensive present.

❧ 2 ❧

Chapter 2

I had a happy and fairly uneventful childhood. Pictures in the family album show me to have been a bun faced little girl with a brace on her teeth.

I went to the local convent school where the nuns were sweet and pious and even forgave me my opening question on the first day of term:

'Are you allowed to be Protestant here?'

I had overheard my parents discussing the denominational factor. As the old saying goes:

'Little pitchers have large ears.'

I can remember that Mother Superior said:

'We are only here to teach you and 90% of education is entirely secular. The religion we teach is only Bible stories and our daily act of worship is very ecumenical.'

She then gave me that saintly fixed smile that I soon learned meant that there were to be no supplementaries. Any idea that nuns were a soft touch on discipline was very quickly dispelled on the first day and I settled down to a quiet and not unpleasant phase of my life.

My father was a lawyer and earned enough in the country town in which we lived to send his daughter first to convent school, then to an expensive boarding school and finally to an even more expensive finishing school. I remember I always wanted to do domestic science, which was all the rage with girls just then, or with those, like me, not clever enough for university. But my mother said, with great firmness. 'No, you can cook very well already, and I'm quite capable of teaching you anything you don't know. Off you go and learn to be a lady.' I learnt to be a lady all right.

Father had fought in the Second World War and was wounded at El Alamein, leading the soldiers of the 5th Indian Division through the German minefields. He was hit by a bullet in his thigh and spent six weeks in hospital.

Mother served in the First Aid Nursing Yeomanry, always called the Fannys, and she followed the victorious American and British armies across the Rhine. They both seemed to have enjoyed their war, in retrospect anyway. If I am bi-sexual, it has nothing to do with anything that happened in my childhood. I thought my mother was pretty but that, I am sure, has nothing to do with it. I am convinced that I am just a chance mutation, that occurs quite naturally, pro rata, in every population. I was not even frightened by a man when I was little, as some of my schoolfriends said they were.

I was carefully and successfully sheltered in a family where sex was never mentioned, and about the most adventurous thing I ever did was hold hands with my boy cousin in the cinema on one special occasion. He wanted to kiss me I think, but was too shy to do so. I got a peck on the cheek instead from an embarrassed schoolboy who just stumbled out his thanks for a pleasant evening. As a matter of fact, I have often thought holding hands is a nice thing to do if you like each other, but we Anglo-Saxons are often too inhibited to do it. The stiff upper lip and all that I suppose. I still like my boy cousin, who is now grown up. We are friends and always will be.

Perhaps though, the stiff upper lip was always our greatest virtue, although it is fashionable to sneer at it these days. I remember my father saying to me once, one summer evening as the corn was coming in from the ripening fields:

'This land is ours, because we were the most ferocious fighting animals the world has ever known. Wherever there is plenty because the land is rich, it is because our forefathers seized it.'

His father fought at Mons, and his grandfather in the South African War, and his great grandfather rode with the Heavy Brigade at Balaclava. The men of our family have always been soldiers. I can remember too, he said he hoped I would marry into the army. I think, perhaps, I was closer to my father than my mother, though I loved her too. We were a happy family in my childhood, and when the sun went down in the west there was peace and contentment in my heart.

One of my earliest memories is of standing at the bathroom window and seeing a great flaming orb in the sky just dipping below the horizon, and saying:

'Mummy, what's that?'

'It's the sun you silly!'

Mother did not suffer fools gladly. But she kissed me goodnight after she had dried my hair, read me my goodnight story, and said:

'You know, your father and I have never had a cross word that amounted to anything.'

My family was super, and I place it on record.

Although the photographs in the family album show me as being plain-pretty at the best, I could not have been too unattractive because, so they tell me, a man unbeknown to us, once borrowed a ladder just to try and peep at me in the bath.

Unhappily for him my grandmother, my father's mother, was staying with us for a week or two and all he saw was granny, for she had decided to have a bath at six o'clock in the evening which was usually my time.

Anyway, the police were told and the unfortunate farmer, whose ladder it was, was not allowed to have it back until it had been finger printed. Someone had stolen it from him for the planned peep through the bathroom window in the dark of a winter's evening and all the Peeping Tom saw was granny in the bath at the age of 56. My father said that granny thought it was very funny and served him right, and I was not told about it until I was grown up, in case I was frightened. My family suspected who it was, a quite ridiculous man in the neighbourhood, who had gone round for years ineffectually alarming women. However the police never got to the bottom of it, nothing could be proved, and now it has all gone down the river of time, as a matter of little consequence.

When I was told about it, years later, my reaction was, well they may say that I was a plain little girl, but someone thought I was pretty enough to carry a wooden ladder two miles in the dark, over a wet ploughed field, just to try and look at me in the bath, the silly old fool.

Mother always said I was vain, and I suppose she was right. But I knew a girl, who went to convent school with me, who was so sure she was uninteresting that she developed a complex about it when, in fact, she was not at all bad-looking. The rush for her when she reached the age of puberty so shocked her sensibilities that she took the veil. Some people are very difficult to please, was all I could say when I was told.

I always liked being admired. Mother said that when I won first prize at the baby show at the church fair I grinned all over my six-month-old face. The runner-up was a baby boy who ended up as a pug ugly prize fighter in a boxing ring.

I was never a problem child and I gave my family no problems at all during my childhood. I was a good little girl and I know that I have over-compensated in later life for my early virtue. But throughout my adult life I have never forgotten the first principles my parents taught me that love is the most important thing in life.

When she thought I was the right age, mother dutifully told me all about the facts of life but in such an obtuse and ladylike way that much of it went right over my head. She even warned me about female homosexuality, although she did not actually say *that*. As I remember it, she told me about a pernicious cult of a Greek woman, who lived in 1500 B.C. and was called Lesbia, which did not register with me at all. She also said something about sapphism.

At 17 my mother had got a job modelling clothes in a London hotel. There she had been propositioned by a rich, middle-aged woman in the ladies' cloakroom. This woman, whose fingers were simply encrusted with diamond rings, she said, took my mother into one of the cubicles, locked the door and got her hand inside the very underclothes that mother was modelling. After a short, sharp struggle, mother escaped but not before she had been offered and refused, a hundred pounds, in those old white £5 notes, to go to the woman's bedroom.

All this I pieced together, with experience, many years later. At the time I did not really understand what she was talking about. No wonder they concluded I was not bright enough for university. Poor mother, it must have been a most unpleasant confrontation, especially as she did not, I think, have any of the inclinations of her wayward daughter. She did her best to warn me of the dangers ahead, but to no avail. I remember thinking that £100 was an awful lot of money just to go and sit with this lady in a hotel bedroom. I mean, what could they do? T.V. had not been invented in those days. Perhaps they would play whist. I assumed she was lonely.

Looking back on it I was not merely naive. I was dim and it is a wonder I survived.

At the time of the incident mother was so upset that she dashed off home, got her bathing costume, and went swimming to feel clean again. I do not know how far this woman got with her jewelled hand, but far enough by the sound of it. Normally mother was the calmest person in the world.

That experience put her right off modelling. She gave notice the next day and put herself down for a secretarial course. That is how she met my father, so it was a lucky decision. But for that woman, Jane would not, perhaps, have come into the world.

I have often wondered whether my personal emotional orientation was anything to do with my father wanting a son as well as a daughter, but I do not think so. I was an only child and was frequently alone when I was young, without being lonely. I was very self-sufficient I suppose. Only children often are.

My father took me everywhere with him, during the holidays, at any rate, so I knew quite a lot about the law by the time I was in my teens. I also learned to shoot and fish and ride, although I was not a good shot. When I was firing at rabbits or pheasants, I was rather pleased when I missed and I was always too soft-hearted to pull the fish out of the water.

But it was my mother who taught me to appreciate music. If it had not been for the war she might have made a career out of the Arts. As it was, the summit of her musical ability was to become a pretty good organist for the local church and to give concerts of organ music for charities and schools.

My memories of my parents were of supreme respectability, but listening to their stories I gathered they had both been moderately wild for a spell in their youth. I was glad of that, because to have been pillars of the Establishment all their lives would have been a tale of monumental dullness. My father was, of course, the most frank.

Men do not mind a little harmless bragging about the amorous activities they got up to; women are rather more reticent about theirs. I am the exception that proves the rule I expect, but even I have the grace to be rather ashamed of myself. One thing I can say, however, is that I have always succeeded in keeping the seamy side of my love life out of my family's knowledge – that is if you exclude my husband, who was not only well aware but intensely interested in my love life. We used to lie in bed discussing it and it never failed to arouse him when I came to the interesting bits. I am told many men have the same reaction as John's to their wives activities, and a few are hostile; probably the inadequate ones. And John was never inadequate. In, or out of bed, my husband was always a winner.

We used to entertain quite a lot and I became quite a reasonable dinner-time conversationalist. Anyway, I often found I could make people laugh with my stories and my mother used to frown if they were too risqué.

'Where did you hear that from?' She would say, which I always recognized as a mark of maternal disapproval.

'One of my girl friends.' I would reply, brightly. I found one of the best ways of passing off a story of doubtful taste was to tell it in dialect. You could get away with murder, even at the most up-market social occasion if you could imitate an Irish brogue or catch the delightful lilt of the soft Welsh tongue. I became quite a mimic, encouraged by my Papa and tolerated, just, by a fairly indulgent, if disapproving, Mama. Mother was not a prude, but I think she thought she owed it to her daughter to exert a moderating influence. If only she knew the wayward wickedness of her only daughter, but she never did. I kept it all to myself. And to John.

Of course, we are led to assume that our mothers have always been the supreme example of maidenly decorum. Sometimes I have wondered how some of my generation ever arrived on the face of the earth. But going through old boxes in the attic one day, I came across a wallet full of photographs of my mother in the nude, aged about 25 or so. One had 'Taken by Bill on his leave, 1941' written on the back of it. And my father's name was not Bill. Feeling guilty, I returned them to the box and fled. After I had got over my acute embarrassment, I found myself saying, 'Well, why not? If my mother was never sexy Jane would never have advanced beyond the twinkle in Dad's eye.' And if mother was sexy with one man, I expect she was like that with others. And she was so pretty I doubt if any sex-starved soldier back from the front could have resisted her charms.

There is a portrait in the drawing room of her in the uniform of the First Aid Nursing Yeomanry which, unlike some of the women's organizations in the last war, was really becoming. There is a funny story which went the rounds I am told, of a soldier coming into a bar and seeing a girl in uniform leaning on it, saying:

'You 'aving one Nurse?'

'No, it's just my ill-fitting uniform.'

The Fanny's uniforms were all tailored in Savile Row, they said, specially for the up-market madams that most of them were. But they were very brave too. Some of them ended up in the gas ovens, having been dropped in plain clothes behind the enemy lines. It paid you to keep quiet about your linguistic abilities I am told, otherwise you were ordered to draw a parachute, and you were droning over the Channel in a Miles Magister monoplane the very next night. Mother could speak excellent French, if rather accented.

'But they let me off,' she said. 'I was afraid of heights.'

Both my parents look so English neither of them could ever have passed themselves off as French or Belgian, particularly mother, who would have been caught straight away because even if her schoolgirl French pronunciation had not betrayed her, her face would have done so. So I was glad she was afraid of heights. Personally, nothing would induce me to jump out of an aeroplane with a parachute, nothing but sheer necessity that is. I even get goose pimples watching people doing it on television, let alone for real.

My father had only one fault, if it was a fault, he loved rugby football, and rugger dinners. For the quiet Englishman he was, he would let himself go on his annual trip to Twickenham – Twickers, as he and his friends called it – to watch the final.

I can always remember my mother's mock horror when Dad returned from his annual outing one year, seven seas under, singing:

'I'm not the pheasant plucker, I'm the pheasant plucker's son and I'm only plucking pheasants till the pheasant plucker comes, and when the pheasant plucker comes and plucks the pheasants here, he'll be the only pheasant plucker you have seen around this year.'

I thought it was funny and I did not share my mother's disapproval. But then, I would always forgive my father anything and getting a little merry after a day out with his friends did not strike me as very reprehensible. Three hundred and sixty-four days of the year he was as sober as the judges he spent his time addressing.

I have not always been butch. In my teens I was femme and I had been used by women as I used women now.

I shall always remember the first time. I was at a boarding school and I was just 16 years of age. The house mistress had told me to sleep in the Tower bedroom, a single room at the head of a gothic tower.

I had just slid into the cold linen sheets, my bedsocks firmly on and my satin nightdress – pretty, but ever so cold – firmly pulled down, when Janice, the head of the house came in.

'Miss Gardner told me to come up and kiss you goodnight,' she explained.

My first thought was, 'How nice of her.' Then I looked at Janice. She seemed to be breathing rather hard, from running up the stairs no doubt. Her bright blonde hair, cut shoulder length with a clasp, as sixth formers were allowed, reflected the glow of the bedside light.

Then she did a funny thing. She took the clasp out of her hair, so it fell down across her face and, leaning forward, untied the thick, pony tail that we younger ones were made to wear. As soon as my hair was spread across the pillow she got into bed with me and, taking me in her arms, kissed me on the mouth, with her tongue flickering in and out. I was shattered. I had never even been kissed by a boy under the mistletoe, let alone by a sex-starved, 18-year-old, girl prefect. I had led a rather protected life, I suppose.

She stayed with me for several hours and by the time she left she had done everything to me one girl could do to another. And I had my first sexual orgasm in her eager, schoolgirl mouth, despite my faint protests.

It was a Thursday night and we bathed, once a week, on Fridays. I said I wanted to wash first but Janice just would not let me. She said she preferred me as I was and I remember that she wrenched apart my thighs, undoing my crossed ankles and then lay for some minutes actually smelling my vagina. Finally she inserted her tongue. I was very excited already, because she had put her fingers up me, and the feeling of a girl's moist tongue sent me through the roof. She told me she was going 'to lick me out' – I had never heard the phrase before – and then proceeded to do so as if I were a jar of cream (which I was, really).

Janice, I remember, wiped me dry with the forelock of her silky, blonde hair. It was quite wet when she had finished, but she clipped it up with her clasp and said:

'I am going off to my bed now and as I masturbate, I will let my hair fall across my face. I shall smell you as I play with myself and think of what I have done to you. Don't you masturbate? Oh, you must. It's great fun. I'll show you how. Next time I come, I'll rub your hair up and down me until it's wet like mine. Then I'll leave you alone and you can try.'

She kissed me and left as swiftly as she had come, and I slept like a log.

It was the first of many visits. I had found a new hobby, a new pastime, something to do other than play hockey and netball and swot up for examinations. Looking back, I remember I used to wait for her visits and be terribly disappointed if she failed to arrive to 'kiss me goodnight'. Who else was she kissing, I would wonder?

It was years before I found out, by accident, talking to another girl after we had left, that there was a lesbian ring at that school led by our house mistress, who had put me in that single, remote tower room to make me available for Janice, one of her ring of older girls. I was sent there because I was thought to be attractive enough to be indoctrinated by Janice. Had I not played ball I would have been back in the dormitory. But I played ball all right! After the first shock of being touched by a girl on my sexual parts, I took to it like a duck to water. I was very femme in those days.

But I might have guessed that Janice's visits had semi-official sanction. She was never hurried. She always stripped me naked when she came and she often stayed half the night. And I had dark shadows under my eyes in the morning. Whenever she could she came on Thursdays, the night before bath night for juniors, when my hair and my armpits and my sexual organs were the most unwashed. She washed me with her tongue. Even sucking my hair clean if she could, sucking it until it was wet. I soon learnt that she liked me better that way, and I never took any particular steps to make myself more presentable before she came.

Sometimes she would come as late as midnight and wake me up. At least once I detected the taste of another girl on her lips when she kissed me, and was insanely jealous. I was not the only one, she told me, when I challenged her, nor would I ever be. I had to take it or leave it and I took it.

Sometimes she would make me kneel down before her and swear I loved her. She would hold me by my long, brown hair wrapped around her fist and tell me to put my tongue inside her. I did not like that at first, but it grew on me. I was always wet and warm myself by the time I was allowed to stop. And I was never allowed to stop until Janice had had enough, enough to bring her to the point of orgasm.

I adored her and grew to live for her nocturnal

visits. Janice played me like a little musical instrument and, looking back on it, she was quite good at her job of seducing schoolgirls. This schoolgirl anyway.

And I did learn to masturbate. One night Janice took my plait and pushed it half up inside her until it was wet and smelling of her. Then she left me. I spread my hair over my hands and buried my face in it, then, removing my right hand, I fingered myself until I climaxed, thinking about Janice. Next morning, I had to rush into the bath room, before anyone woke up, to wash my hair clean. Happily, it was raining, so then I went outside and got soaking wet so I could go to Matron to have my hair dried officially. One of the school rules was that girls were not allowed to sit around with wet hair if they had been out in the rain. I was terrified that someone might guess my sin. But nobody did, of course.

Janice gave me every privilege. I was 'excused games' whenever I wanted and soon became known as one of her 'pets'. I suppose the other pets played ball too. I noticed that they were all pretty 16 and 17-year-olds. One of them appeared one morning with her long, fair hair soaking wet and was told to go to Matron and have it dried. I wondered if Janice had done the same to her. I never found out. But I tested her by kissing her when we were out for a walk that afternoon and she let me, so I was probably right.

In due course, school came to an end and I was packed off by my parents to a finishing school in

Switzerland, half way up a mountain. There I shared a room with a girl a year older than me called Claire, who was so beautiful I found myself hoping she was a lesbian like me – I had just looked up the word in the dictionary. I hoped she was but it was too much to hope, I concluded.

That evening we were dancing together, as we had to every day, and she touched my breast. I removed her hand, only to find it back there a minute later. In the half light of the furthest alcove I submitted, willingly, to her kiss. She was so lovely, Claire, with a lithe, strong Nordic figure, and straight, rich hair which she wore long and loose. Mine was shoulder length by now. She was German and she looked so feminine. But she was the one on top, she made the running. She climbed into bed with me that very night, behind locked doors, and made love to me like the expert she was. She said all German girls had lesbian affairs, as well as having boys.

After that we always slept together, half the night in one bed and half in the other. When we moved over I was always underneath again, and Claire was moving suggestively on top of me. Except when the cycle of our female bodies precluded it, we made love at least twice every night. And even when she could not go further she used to kiss me until I got uncomfortable and had to get up and change. I did not enjoy that but there was no arguing with Claire. I once said I understood Hitler better since I had met her. She laughed and said, 'Nonsense, you like it!' And generally speaking I did too.

I shall always remember the rich, warm smell

of her body, her insistent hands and her strong demanding mouth. Funnily enough, we were not great friends during the day, it was only when night came that we fitted together like a jigsaw puzzle. I suppose we were just two randy teenagers without boys. Although, for me, it was more than that. I would have been quite lost without Claire, or if not Claire, somebody. I wonder what has happened to Claire now? I never saw her after finishing school.

Claire had to sleep alone one night though. In the winter we went skiing and, one evening, I found myself at the top of the ski lift with Frau Grisel Gunter, the games and skiing mistress. As we were about to get on the lift – we were the last left on top of the mountain – it suddenly stopped. After some time we realized it had stopped for the night. The Swiss had a system to cope with this. You stayed in a little hut, with all modern conveniences, until the first lift in the morning.

I remember thinking it all rather fun. We went to the hut, lit the fire and all the lamps provided, then went round drawing all the curtains on the double-glazed windows and locking up.

As we did so I noticed Grisel kept on bumping into me or reaching over my shoulder to help me lock a door or window and pressing up to me. For a brief while I thought little of it. She was 40, and I was 17, and in great awe and respect of her as staff.

Then suddenly I knew. She buried her face in my hair from behind me and said how nice it smelt. Then, clasping my already quite large breasts in her two hands, she made unmistakeable movements up and down my bottom.

She let me go but I knew the score by now. Several times more she caught and handled me and my pants were quite wet by the time she trapped me against a wall with a table either side. She lifted my hair with her hands then suddenly gripped it hard, pulling my face towards her. Then she kissed me on the lips, rubbing herself up and down me. I felt weak and gave in to her. I liked it anyway, but had never thought of her in that context. She was grown up, sex was for kids.

But I had sex with her that night. We lay naked, side by side in front of a roaring fire, and she literally licked me from head to foot. She was a German Swiss and very thorough. But she was also very good at it. Someone told me afterwards she had had more women and girls than any man in her canton. Certainly she seemed to have had most of the girls at my finishing school, quite a number of whom had missed the last ski lift with her. I was quite a little celebrity in the morning. They all knew what must have happened – and it had of course.

I remember I got so excited at the licking that, when she followed with her hand, I literally let her put her whole hand inside me. Then she lay on top of me between my legs and I found that her clitoris, which stuck out from her pubic hair like a penis, actually penetrated. I climaxed, willingly, all over it and she called me a 'sexy little English miss'.

I went to sleep with my head on her ample bosom, cuddled up and happy and was done again for luck, as she put it, in the morning. She took her sex very cheerfully, I remember. But she brooked no argument. What she said went and I was never once asked if I wanted to. I formed the impression that she expected surrender and I did not care to find out what would happen if I refused.

She questioned me closely about Claire. It is difficult not to answer truthfully when a woman has her hand half way up you, so I told her everything. And she wanted to know everything, right down to the last detail.

A week later, Claire was missing from our bedroom, and in the morning I had to help to comb out tangles from her long, silky hair. She had spent the night with Grisel. And not on top.

After that she was missing from time to time. And always with the skiing mistress. Each time she came back she just cuddled me for a couple of days. It was as if she was sexually exhausted by Grisel. Perhaps she was.

One evening that first winter, Claire came into our room with Grisel, who locked the door and undressed. She was a good looking brunette, powerfully built with pendulous, heavy breasts, prominent nipples and with a pink clitoris standing erect out of her thick bush of pubic hair. She got into bed, not with Claire, but with me, pulling Claire in after her.

She lay on top of me, with Claire beside me and I distinctly felt her clitoris slide into me. I thought, 'this must be what a boy feels like'.

By the time Grisel was finished it was my turn to be exhausted. She made love to me, on and off, all night. And when she was not, she encouraged Claire to do so too.

And in the morning she took Claire as well. She left us both at 6 a.m. and we slept on and missed our breakfasts.

Then, of course, we were late on the ski slopes. Grisel actually gave us both a public reprimand. As a cover-up exercise it was fine, but I remember feeling it was a bit overdone.

'Claire,' she said, 'I don't intend being kept waiting by you! And tuck your hair in. It may be pretty, but there is a time for everything. If you can't look tidy on the ski slope, I will make you cut it all off. And you, Jane, hold yourself up. You look as if you have been on the roof with a man all night. And tuck your hair in too. This is a ski slope parade, not a line up of call girls outside a brothel.' Giggles came from all the others. Half of them had had Grisel on top of them in bed, and probably guessed why we were getting the sharp end of her tongue. She was like a barnyard rooster crowing on a muck heap. I felt like crying. 'Bitch,' said Claire, under her breath, 'I won't let her again.'

Nevertheless, it was a week before Claire took me again. It was just cuddles till then. Poor Claire, because she was butch, she had had a harder time with Grisel than I did. The ski mistress had been almost vindictive in the violence of her love making with the girl who was, despite her sexual sophistication, only 18. Claire showed me the whip marks on her bottom and I gasped.

'Did you like that?' I said.

'No,' replied Claire, 'but she did.'

'Why did you let her then?'

'You try stopping a German Swiss on heat!'

But I think she enjoyed the scene as a whole, because there was no doubt she always returned sexually exhausted by Grisel's activities. And you do not get replete unless you actually like it.

❦ 3 ❦

Chapter 3

Believe it or not, Claire was also interested in boys and, through her, I met my first real date.

I was surprised to find that I was not a lesbian really, or so I concluded, because I found boys fun. I even enjoyed their sexual advances, although I was careful not to let them go too far, in case I had to be sent home pregnant and in disgrace, as had happened to a girl from a good home a few years ago. The school was nearly closed down over the scandal Claire warned me.

I did not need the warning. I had read all the books about the birds and the bees.

One evening I was lying on the beach in the moonlight with a boy. Claire with her boy lay a few yards away and as I was kissing my boy, I found myself thinking of Claire. This was disturbing. I was meant to be thinking about the boy who was petting me enthusiastically. When I climaxed he was so pleased with himself, not knowing that it was Claire who had really given me the orgasm, and not this young Italian Swiss waiter with whom we had climbed out of our room to go midnight bathing.

Later on, in our room I told Claire.

'You are silly,' she said. 'Come here.'

When I responded to her advances I could not help thinking, 'I suppose I am bi-sexual really, but so far I really prefer girls.'

The next day I resolved not to worry about it. I liked men, I liked their company and if, when they made love to me, I found myself making love with a girl in my secret thoughts well then, so what? I wasn't going to turn myself into a nervous wreck with worry. I would take my pleasure where it came and keep my thoughts to myself, I reasoned. Boys were for having babies with. I granted they were essential for that but, apart from getting married one day and raising a family, I was not particularly enamoured with men sexually.

But then I fell in love. He was a soldier on leave from Germany and he joined the ski class for special tuition. I thought he was wonderful from the first moment I saw him. His name was John Roberts and he was a captain in a line regiment. The other officers of his unit called him Jack, he told me.

We saw each other only under strict supervision, and his week's leave was up before it had started. Or so it seemed. When he said goodbye he kissed Claire too, and a pang of jealousy turned my stomach upside down. So I knew I was in love.

The trouble was I was in love with Claire too.

That night, when we cuddled, I got on top of Claire. She let me pet her for a bit and then took over. But I suddenly realized I wanted to be the sexual aggressor. But so did Claire. For the moment I accepted the situation but, often, as Claire was making love to me I was mentally making love to her! In my mind I was the one on top. I came to the conclusion, probably accurately, that I was a mixed-up kid. A three way mixed-up girl. But then imagination, I remember thinking, is what makes us so different from the rest of the animal kingdom. And I had plenty of imagination.

John wrote to me, of course, and I to him. I used to rush downstairs for his letters in the morning and be most disappointed when there were none. I was generally lucky, because we wrote to each other every day, and it was only an accident of the postal services which occasioned the gaps.

I had his photograph by my bed. It revealed a square-jawed humorous face, light brown hair and blue eyes. I used to think he was every inch a soldier. I was determined to marry him.

It was not a long courtship. We were married in the spring, a few months after leaving finishing school. We spent our honeymoon in the Canary Isles.

Sex was not everything I found. Life was 90% *not* sex, I concluded philosophically, so why fuss about it so much? John and I got on very well together, we laughed at the same things, we enjoyed the same food and we had similar views on the arts, politics and the world. And he, being just five years older than me, took charge with just enough enthusiasm to indulge my latent laziness and not enough to irritate my dormant feminism.

I told him a little about my liking for girls, bit by bit and very carefully. Slowly it dawned on me that he did not mind that at all. He could be jealous over other men, but not over women.

'I might be a bit fed up if I just didn't like the woman', he said, 'but you wouldn't like it if one of my chums was a 'Mark One' stinker, would you?'

Everything comes to an end eventually, and the end of our honeymoon came all too soon. It had been fun, particularly the part we spent in bed together, and I concluded that I enjoyed making love with John. He was gentle and considerate, if a trifle lacking in imagination. I made up for that of course, and found myself indulging in fantasy whenever I wanted to climax. And the fantasy, I noticed, was always another girl. I resolved not to fight my perverse urges, but swim along with them.

In Germany we were given the usual fairly pleasant quarters for an officer of my husband's rank, and settled down to an army social life.

I found my husband's brother officers friendly and amusing, and some of their wives disturbingly attractive; but, mindful of John's career, I behaved as if butter would not melt in my mouth.

Then, in the social club we both belonged to, I met Maria. She was in her forties, the widow of a control commission official who had settled permanently in Germany, and spoke the language fluently.

We knew each other for what we were the moment our eyes met. Even so, it was a long time before we broached the subject but every time we were in the same room, she sought me out and was excessively friendly. I liked her too.

She was tall and slim, with hair thick, very dark and flecked with grey. Elegant and beautifully dressed, she always attracted attention I noticed. Her grey eyes were steel when she was angry, but soft when she spoke to me.

Eventually she asked me to spend a weekend with her at her second home in the Bavarian Alps.

'I do want you to meet my teenaged daughter,' she said. 'You would love her. She is so pretty.'

My heart missed a beat. What was I being invited to? Did I mistake her meaning?

That weekend, with John away on army exercises, I accepted her invitation and we drove off in her Mercedes to the distant hills.

She talked a lot about her daughter Jill as we drove along. She had her hand on my leg for most of the time, but it was not until we were nearly there that she stopped in a lay-by and kissed me. From her kiss I knew what the form would be. There was no need for words. I was to do as I was told. As I returned her kiss I said I would, also without words. It had been a long time since I had been kissed by a lesbian, for that is what I knew she was, and I was hungry for a new experience. The way I felt I was game for anything. But, I wondered, exactly what had she in mind?

I was soon to find out.

The snow was falling softly on the ground as we drove up to the chalet, set on the side of a mountain, and screened from the road by tall fir trees.

Jill, having arrived from school by taxi, opened the door to us. She was, as her mother had said, very pretty, with straight red-gold hair cascading to the middle of her back, held back by an Alice band. She looked about 16 but I never did discover her real age. She was old enough to drink wine, a glass of which she had already poured out for herself.

Mother and daughter kissed affectionately, and when I was introduced Maria said:

'There, isn't she lovely?'

'You are embarrassing her,' I replied, 'but she is, of course. I wish I were her age again. I had such fun at school.'

'Did you?' said Jill. 'What did you do?'

'You'd be surprised!' I replied with a smile. 'I'll tell you later.'

It was a beautiful house, furnished with heavy antique German furniture down to the usual cuckoo clock, fitted carpets, heavy drapes and double glazing everywhere. A roaring log fire completed the scene and added to the general impression of warmth, comfort and privacy.

Jill came and sat on the floor beside my chair. She did not look very like her mother. At first I thought she might be Maria's daughter, until I discovered she was her stepdaughter. But she was a lovely child, whatever the relationship.

From the start I realized that I was expected to seduce her. Maria held the view, not uncommon on the Continent she said, that lesbianism was a marvellous substitute for boys, and kept a teenaged daughter safe until she was of a marriageable age.

Later in the evening taped music was switched on and Maria suggested we dance.

'Dance in the old-fashioned way,' she told us. And I gathered Jill in my arms and danced dreamily round the room with her. Maria came up and removed Jill's Alice band so her hair flowed free, and then took the pin out of my hair so it fell forward. To please Maria I danced cheek-to-cheek and body-to-body. Greatly daring, I kissed her daughter on the mouth when I was at the side of the room furthest away from the mother. Then, when I was opposite her mother, the lights went out. I put my hand inside the girl's dress and felt her smooth, soft and tiny breasts.

'Can I sleep with you tonight?' I asked her.

'Yes, if Mama will let you,' she replied. 'There are only two bedrooms, so we have to double up somehow. They are both double beds.'

I kissed her again, pulling the shoulder straps of her dress down so that, as the lights went up, it was quite obvious where my hand had been. I led her towards Maria who said:

'She's tired. It is about time you took the child to bed. Jane. She'll never get up in the morning otherwise.'

I needed no second invitation and swept her off to bed without further ceremony.

'See she cleans her teeth,' were the last words I heard. 'Jill is rather inclined to leap into bed unwashed, unbrushed and with her clothes all over the floor.'

'I'll pick up her clothes anyway,' I told Maria, giving Jill a playful pat on the bottom.

As I closed the door behind us I gathered the girl up and lifted her in the air in my arms.

'I'll clean your teeth and wash you all over once I've got you into bed and not before. So there!' She sighed. 'I don't mind, Jane, what you do. I am glad you are sleeping with me and not Mama.'

I wondered. How sophisticated was this girl? Was I the first to take her to bed or just one of many? Maria was a strange character. I had not fathomed her yet by any means. But if she wanted her schoolgirl daughter seduced, I needed no prompting.

We were both in bed together in the nude in three seconds and I didn't pick up her clothes. She had a lovely little figure and we wrapped ourselves round each other with as little hesitation as if we had been told to do it. Which, of course, was the truth of the matter. I kissed her little breasts taking the nipples in my mouth. Her body smelt warm and scented and she was eager for my caresses. She looked so young and pretty lying in my arms that I would have felt guilty if I had not been so excited by her presence. After all, if Maria did not mind, why should I? But she is a strange mother I thought. I put my arm under her long fair hair and spread it over the pillow.

'I love you Jill,' I said without a great deal of insincerity. She was so adorable at that moment it was impossible not to love her. The Greeks had many words for love, not just one like us. It was one of the Greek versions I expect I really meant as I threaded my fingers through the girl's soft pubic hair. I could feel the heat from her as I did so. I buried my face in her hair and said, 'Open your legs, you'll sleep better if I pet you first. That was one thing I learnt at school, although school seems a long time ago now.'

Obediently she did as I asked and my fingers slid up inside her. She was quite ready for me. Ready and very eager. I gripped one of her legs between mine and felt a wave of relief as my flesh touched hers. She was not the only one who was ready and eager. It was mutual.

In the darkness of her room we clung together, locked in each other's arms. And the girl's mother, who had engineered it all, lay only a few yards away in the next room.

'I suppose she gets a thrill out of it,' I thought.

The next morning, after Jill had gone off to school, her mother slipped into her daughter's bedroom.

'This is when I pay for my night's lodgings,' I thought. And I was right. Marie untied her dressing gown and got into bed with me. As she made love to me she said:

'Was she all right?'

'She was heaven.' I replied. 'But I was very gentle with her, I just cuddled her.'

After we had made love several times Maria said:

'Be my permanent girl friend. Come down here and you can have Jill every time you want. I'll even let you take the child's virginity with one of those things if you like.'

'No, I could never hurt her!' I replied.

'Well, if you won't take her virginity I will,' said Maria in a strange voice. Then I realized she was having an orgasm. Both her legs were clasped round one of mine.

Later she admitted that thought of raping her young daughter was only a masturbation fantasy and that she would never, actually, do it.

'But you would have let me!' I replied.

'Yes, I would have let you,' she said.

Months later I met a woman in the club who knew Maria. She said: 'She is a queer woman. Jill is not her daughter, she's her step-daughter. Apparently the girl's mother, who was very beautiful, ran off and left her father who, to his last breath, was still in love with his wife. That is why poor Jill, who I think is 18 not 16, is kept dressed very young and is offered to any woman who will take her, as a sort of revenge on the first wife. I wouldn't be surprised if Maria puts her on the streets when she leaves school.'

I went there once more and had Jill again. She really did look 16 and had an adolescent's mannerisms. But she made love like a dream and, sorry for the girl though I was, I took full advantage of her step-mother's generosity. If she was on offer it might as well be me as some heavy German frau.

'She will get that, too, next week.' I remember thinking as I pushed the girl's mouth towards my vagina. Jill was good at making love that way too and it was quite obvious that I was not the first woman to introduce her to that particular sexual act. I wondered if her step-mother had broken her in.

I asked Maria about it next day, as I was lying in her arms.

'Yes, of course I did,' she said. 'Someone else would have done it if I hadn't. Actually, I pretended it was a punishment for talking to a boy out of her bedroom window, but she was going to get it anyway. She has never looked back since then.'

'I would like to watch you.' I replied.

'Stay another night and you can,' said Maria.

That night I shared a bed with both of them and watched step-mother and step-daughter in the full act of lesbian sex, the Circle of Venus.

'I taught her that ages ago,' said Maria after Jill had climaxed under her step-mother's experienced tongue.

Jill seemed to be quite happy in bed with two older women both intent on having sex with her. So, perhaps, Maria was not really being as unkind to her little ward as, mentally, she would have liked to have been. Lesbian sex is very twisted sometimes. 'It is all in the mind,' one woman once said to me.

Jill was excused school the next day. We were at her all night. And I was every bit as bad as her step-mother. I think we both egged each other on. The girl was physically and sexually exhausted by the morning. If she had been sent to school she would have dropped asleep at her lessons.

I was a bit tired myself.

John tells me that there are brothels for women in Hamburg where any middle-aged woman can have the choice of a boy or a girl and the girls are twice the price of the boys.

'Why?' I asked.

'I suppose because boys quite like being fiddled about with by an older woman but there are not many young girls who can be induced to go with any raddled old matron who happens to take a fancy to their hips.'

If Maria has heard of them, then that, I fear, is where her step-daughter is going to fetch up. And I would not put it past her to send Jill's real mother a free ticket.

I have never met a more determined woman than Maria. I can still see, in my mind's eye, her thick, dark, greying hair falling over and mingling with Jill's fair hair on the pillow as she prised the girl's legs apart. She was the epitome of the dominant female and she practically owned Jill. It was the relationship of mistress and sex object rather than mother and daughter.

But what will, undoubtedly save Jill is that her step-mother's very possessiveness will preclude her ever being allowed a life of her own.

However, you never know, perhaps some Prince or Princess Charming will come along.

And, of course, once Maria reaches a certain age, not too far off, she may well lose all interest in sex, straight or otherwise. Then Jill will be free at last. I hope so anyway, because she is a sweet girl and I feel almost guilty at my part in the affair. But if it had not been me it would have been another. There had been others.

However let no one assume that Jill did not participate willingly. She enjoyed it sexually and was quite well aware of what she was about. I suppose most teenagers, if encouraged as she was, would be just about the same. Look at me for instance, there was every school rule to stop me, but I was in there pitching just the same. But Jill was wise beyond her years on the subject of lesbianism. As she said to me in bed, just before she went off to school after that first night:

'Mummy told me what to do and I did it. I was the lure, you were the quarry and my mother was the predator. And when I saw you I was glad you were so pretty. Often they are not and then it takes a bit longer to turn me on. I sometimes wonder what Mummy sees in some of them.'

That was when I knew what my role was to be once Jill was out of the door. But Maria told me what the plain ones were for. They were just butch dykes she had picked up in lesbian bars and they served no other purpose than that of the humiliation of Jill. I am sure she got a sexual thrill out of that alone. I saw one of the women who had gone to bed with Jill. Maria brazenly pointed her out to me as one of Jill's many lovers. All I can say is, I would not have wanted to sit in the same railway carriage as *that* one, let alone go to bed with her. She looked more like a Prussian field engineer than a woman and even had a duelling scar on one cheek. It had probably been done with a broken bottle in a beer cellar fight.

'I wonder how long she took to turn Jill on,' I said.

'I don't suppose she even bothered,' retorted Maria, 'with a girl as young and lovely as Jill I expect she just amused herself. I told her not to bother to be particularly nice to the child and she is not the sort of woman who would want to be anyway. But I expect Jill got turned on. She is pretty sexy and all cats are black in the dark. Helga said she climaxed alright.'

'I wonder you dared to let her get her hands on her,' I remarked indignantly.

'That was the whole idea. When Helga gets her hands on a girl she knows just what she is doing. She's a hard case.'

'You don't deserve someone like Jill.'

'Well you enjoyed her in bed, didn't you? Where do you think she learned all that? Helga taught her. Helga and some others. I couldn't undertake all her training myself. Mind you I did quite a lot of it. The sophisticated bits.' Maria laughed. She was a good-looking woman. I had enjoyed her lovemaking but there was something about her that I saw in her face at that moment that repelled me.

I enjoyed sleeping with John the next night. Maria nearly turned me off lesbianism. Nearly, but not quite.

Funnily enough, outside the sexual arena, Maria was very kind to her step-daughter. Sumptuous presents, ample pocket money and beautiful clothes, albeit rather too young for her, were showered upon Jill, who, in return, was most affectionate.

Even on the sexual front, Jill preferred her stepmother's bed to any other and was never reluctant to go to it. And anyone who had seen her perform there, as I had, would have said the girl was sexually attracted to Maria. Whether she volunteered to submit to Helga is another matter. The woman was built like a prize-fighter and the question is purely academic. But I expect she did. Jill was very obedient and Maria had instilled the spirit of submission in her.

So, although the world would say it was all pretty sordid, it is, perhaps, wrong to enter into too strict a judgement. Jill lived in a gilded cage, from which, if the door were thrown open she might well have declined to take wing. Some birds prefer their cage and some slaves their servitude.

In short, I think Jill enjoyed almost everything that was done to her and, cynically, no one could say she had had a deprived childhood.

Nevertheless, at the end, I was left with the feeling that I had eaten far too much marzipan.

My last thoughts, as I drifted off to sleep with my arms round John, were of Maria's kind offer to let me take her step-daughter's virginity. I doubt if any girl who had spent a night in Helga's bed could be a virgin. I never thought of checking when I had had the chance.

Some months later I met my acquaintance in the club and she said:

'Have you heard the latest about Jill?'

'No,' I replied, 'I haven't seen Jill or Maria for some time. Maria does not seem to come to the club very often these days. Or if she does it is on different days to me.'

'Well,' she said, 'Jill had a tiff with Maria and decided to run away. Typical teenage rebellion, I imagine. I was told, and this only hearsay, that she wanted to find her real mother. So she hit on the mad idea of asking Helga to help her. Helga said that if she would go to bed with her and another old butch dyke for money, she would see she was all right and pay her fare to America, where she believed her mother was living. The silly thing never thought of asking for her money first, and in the morning, they not only refused to pay her a single mark for her services, but they drove her back by car and handed her over to Maria, who took her upstairs, I expect, and suppressed the rebellion in bed.'

There are some hard people in this world and Maria is one of them. Superficially she is attractive, she attracted me, but when you get to know her well she is like a very beautiful, coloured apple with a worm inside.

I sometimes wonder if Jill went to Helga because she knew she would be returned to base and she did not really want to run away. I know them both so well I can almost read their thoughts. Jill would enjoy having her rebellion suppressed in bed and I know just how Maria would have done it.

Thomas Grey wrote of 'The servitude that hugs her chain.' That was Jill, I am afraid.

4

Chapter 4

There came the time when my husband was up for promotion and, like most wives, I shared his anxiety.

The regiment was away on the frontier on routine exercises, when I received an invitation from the Colonel's lady to drinks.

I arrived, bathed and groomed to the last degree, but dressed informally as the invitation requested. I was surprised to be greeted by Emma, the Colonel's wife, clad in silk pyjama trousers from the waist downwards, and what appeared to be one of her husband's old shirts covering her bosom.

She was a handsome woman of about 45, with prematurely grey hair and a lithe, slim figure. Most of the army wives were frightened of her, and I was no exception. She was a formidable woman by any standards.

We went on to the balcony for drinks and sat on a sofa watching the sun go down, overlooking a forest of pine trees. Emma did most of the talking and eventually she got round to the subject of my husband's promotion. She lent over and touched the back of my neck. 'No one ever gets promoted in this regiment except through me,' she said. I drew my breath in sharply and tried to look alarmed. She had come to the right girl this time, but I was not going to let her know it too soon.

Slowly, she enveloped me in her arms as I made ineffectual squeaks of protest, taking care not to avert my face from hers. When she kissed me, as she did as soon as she had pushed me back along the sofa and had slid on top of me, I returned her kiss. We lay there, in the gathering darkness, for nearly an hour, as she kissed and petted me.

'Stay the night,' she begged, and I said 'I will if I can ring up my girl Sue, she always waits up for me, and she'll ring the police if I don't get home. She's very loyal.'

We were allowed a maid 'on the strength' and, instead of the usual German girl, I had brought a 19-year-old from Dorset. Sue was very useful and very pretty, but I had kept off her because you cannot get the best out of your staff if you mix business and pleasure.

'There is a phone in the bedroom. You can phone from there.'

Emma slid her fingers more firmly inside me, almost possessively. I tried to look very young and defenceless in an older woman's arms, but I was enjoying myself and Emma knew I was, because her fingers and my mouth told her so. I was determined to give her what she wanted but make her feel that she had seduced me.

'In the morning you won't know why you did

this,' said Emma, 'but I shall remind you.' The Colonel's lady was good at this sort of thing, she had probably had a lot of practice, but there was something unpleasant about her. She could take a girl and get her to give everything and then make her feel cheap with remarks like that.

'Oh well, ' I thought, 'that's how the cookie crumbles.' I returned her kiss with passion and accepted her tongue in my mouth.

Once we were in the bedroom and she had undressed me, I asked to use the phone. 'In a minute,' she said pushing me down on the bed and inserting one slim, nude leg between mine. She had slipped out of her clothes, what there was of them, in ten seconds flat.

Half an hour later, at the point of climax, Emma dialled Sue. To my surprise they were soon talking in terms of the greatest intimacy and it then became apparent that, on her days off, she had been in bed with Emma.

And I had never guessed for one minute that they had even met.

'Your mistress wants to speak to you!' The phone was put in my hand and, breathing rather hard, I said I would not be coming back that night.

'Why, what will you be doing Jane?' replied Sue impertinently. She had never used my Christian name before. I was Mrs Roberts.

Emma took the phone from me and said 'She's going to be seduced by me. Why don't you come and join us? You've got a key.'

She replaced the telephone and put her mouth

to mine. 'A threesome with little Sue,' I thought. 'Oh, well, I shall enjoy it, even if it is imprudent.'

A few minutes later the door opened and Sue came in. I was lying under Emma, my arms around her, my legs open.

Sue, having shed her clothes, came and stood beside the bed. 'They have planned this,' I thought, as Emma turned my face towards Sue's pubic hair, and pressed me towards her. She smelt hot and sexy and she had more hair down there than I would have imagined. And I used to imagine. Like a man, I always 'undressed' every women I ever met who had any pretensions to beauty. Her pubic hair was thick and dark and my mouth was pressed to it. Slowly Sue put one leg over my face, aided by a solicitous Emma, who raised herself up from me to allow Sue to sit on my face. Sue's wide open vagina almost enveloped my mouth. She was only 19, but she was all woman. I put my tongue inside, as Emma slid down my body to put her mouth on my genitals. I climaxed not once but two or three times, the last coinciding with Sue, who nearly suffocated me with the intensity of the grip of her firm young thighs.

Actually, it was one of the best threesomes I had ever taken part in. I do not know whether Sue was trying to take her lost wages out of my body, I did not pay her a great deal, or whether she had always fancied her mistress. Whichever way it was, it worked, and we all had a pleasant and rather amusing breakfast together a few hours later.

It was a lovely summer that year. We two were

young and neither of us had any regrets. Even Emma was kind and kept her barbed tongue to herself.

John was promoted, to his satisfaction, a month later. And he never knew how I had helped. He was a good soldier, 'I expect he'd have made it anyway,' I remember thinking. But I never leave anything to chance.

Sue and I became lovers after that night. I soon reversed the roles and became butch, and she was femme. It would have been ridiculous otherwise. I took her every night I wanted her and, when she married a soldier a year later, I went to her wedding and smiled into her eyes as she stood beside her young husband in her white wedding dress. She knew what I was thinking. I had trained her, and in more ways than one. And so had Emma of course.

Poor Sue, I was really rather fond of her. And I do not usually get very fond of women. I tend to use them as a man does, as often as not without any real affection. I suppose that is what makes me a lesbian and, without boasting, a fairly successful one. I have never made a pass at a girl and failed in my life. Perhaps it is true that I do not advance until I am nearly sure, and that is a question of judgment, but, so far, I have always made the girl once I have firmly decided to do so. And, as with a man, the thrill of conquest is always there. At the second of her orgasm in my mouth, or under my hand, I despise her. Once I have cuddled her all night, there is a certain feeling of friendship, of comradeship, but it often does not go very deep. I am a predatory animal where other women are concerned. I once summed up my feelings thus: 'the younger and prettier, the better.' That, and that only. But I liked Sue. She gave me a lot. And I took it.

Those were my feelings up to the time I really got to know Diana. She changed my attitude to life a great deal and, above all, she taught me that friendship between women is not always eroded by a night of perverted sex – for that is what it really is I suppose.

John had a sister, Diana, just five years older than me, with whom I had always got on very well. We laughed at the same stories and I had always thought her a super sister-in-law. She looked a bit like a female version of my husband. You certainly could see they were brother and sister. Diana had been in the Army and was now an executive director of a London merchant bank.

Imagine my surprise when John told me his sister was the same sort of person I was.

'I know she is,' said John, 'but I have never been able to find out anything about her. Why don't you let her seduce you and tell me all about it?'

'Would you want me to?' I replied. 'That's practically incest isn't it? Besides I'm butch.'

'Well you'll just have to pretend to be femme, because I suspect that Diana won't play that role.'

It was arranged that while my husband was away on a weapons' training course, Diana would come and stay and keep me company.

I prepared the ground very carefully and when my sister-in-law arrived at 9 o'clock at night, by taxi from the airport, I was in a nightdress and négligé, with my freshly washed hair loose and unclipped in a good imitation of a fashionable schoolgirl hair style. I hoped that I did not look too much like mutton dressed as lamb.

Diana kissed me on the cheek and said: 'I could do with a drink!'

I poured her a stiff whisky, which is what she wanted, and for me a glass of gin and tonic. I had turned the lights low, had scented myself to the last degree and tried to look provocative, without it being too obvious – a difficult task with another woman.

Diana was dressed in a suit, rather severely cut, with her very dark brown, shoulder length hair well tucked up.

As I gave her her drink she caught hold of my wrist and pulled me down beside her.

'Jane,' she said, 'it's about time we got to know each other a little better. You are my little sister now, you know. And I have always had a soft spot for you.'

I thought: 'It's working. Well, let her make the most of it because I am quite willing. We might as well keep it in the family. John will be most interested in my report on his sister.'

I smiled at Diana and touched her hair. Diana said: 'I'll comb it down for you if you like. This is just for travelling.'

As soon as she had done so she turned and kissed me, this time on the lips. By my response the scene was set. Diana's hand was soon inside my low cut nightie, fondling my breasts.

I thought a tiny protest was in order, just for appearances.

'We can't do this, it's incestuous lesbianism.'

'Yes, isn't it fun,' said Diana with a giggle. 'I always wanted to find out what my brother's wife was like. So, now show me.'

Half an hour and a few long kisses later we were in the guest room, quietly undressing and obviously intent on sharing the same bed. I had very little to do and was helping Diana, when she sat down in a chair and pulled me to her knees in front of her.

'Wet my pubic hair with your tongue and then shave me,' she demanded right out of the blue. Nothing if not direct, was Diana. That's why I had always liked her. I looked at the mass of very dark hair presented to me and obediently, after a moment's hesitation, just to look ladylike, applied my lips. After all, I liked this.

As I licked her Diana explained she was going to do the same to me afterwards.

'You will be surprised the difference it makes. We shall both be really nude. And I shall be able to see what your cunt really looks like.'

Diana had been a girl soldier and she used words like that when she felt like it. After I had licked her for about five minutes I was handed a razor and I proceeded to shave her. Then she did the same for me. I nearly climaxed at least once but Diana removed her tongue just before I did. Then we stood up and looked at each other. Personally, I thought we both looked quite ridiculous but there was something sensuous about it, just the same.

'What am I going to tell my husband?' I said. 'He liked my pubic hair.'

'Tell him you shaved it off to make it grow thicker, because that's what it does.' Diana giggled and so did I, we sounded like the little girls we certainly were not but, shaved as we were, the two of us were rather reminiscent of our distant childhoods.

Once we were in bed we discovered that neither one of us wanted to dominate the other all the time, or rather we both wanted to do it some of the time. We took it in turn to pet each other and I mounted Diana before she did it to me, although it was she that put me there and with my legs apart.

The feeling of naked genitals together was quite extraordinary. We were 1/16th of an inch closer to each other sexually, I suppose, and we could see everything of each other without peering through the undergrowth, as Diana put it.

I think my sister-in-law and I discovered, that night, what the feminists mean when they talk about the sisterhood of lesbianism. We were sisters, we were being very sexy and we had orgasms half the night, with giggles in between, before going to sleep as the dawn light stole through the drawn curtains.

'Let's play spoons.' said Diana, turning me away from her and cuddling me to her. 'I'm tired.' We drifted off to sleep with Diana's hand lying protectively over my naked cunt, as she insisted on calling it. I did not care. I loved Diana and I still do. We have never made love since that one night but we are still great friends and we still laugh at the same things. Diana shares a flat with an 18-year-old ballerina who worships her. I am sure she is very nice to the girl because she is a nice woman.

John was amazed when I told him all. But he has never let Diana know that he knows what she is like. Or that he is well aware that she and his wife have made love together. It excites him though. He once even told me he would have liked to have made love to Diana himself and that he envies me for having done so.

My husband had only one complaint. When my pubic hair had just started to grow again, he remarked that it was like making love to a porcupine. But it was very much thicker and curlier when it was back to normal and John likes it that way, so I suppose it was worth it.

❧ 5 ❧

Chapter 5

Fair as the dawn, her fine, flaxen hair reflecting the light of the room like a cascade of silk, Rosamund was an English beauty. Tall and slender, as graceful as the winter willow in the northern equinoxial breeze, she was so reserved and self-sufficient, that the world seemed to freeze at her finger tips.

It was lust at first sight, as far as I was concerned, but my friendly approach met with no response. She was the wife, I discovered, of a young officer in a smart infantry regiment, presently on secondment.

I met him at a dance when he came over on leave. He was not my type but he was as friendly as his wife was reticent.

I made a dead set at him and later, when he asked me to dance I thrust my leg between his in a certain way which has always turned men on, I have noticed. After a while I could feel, through my evening dress and his dress trousers, that it was working like a charm. He kissed me as we danced behind the inevitable palms and I kissed him back in the way I usually reserve for women.

We sat the next dance out, in the back of his car, and he tried to make me, as men always do if you lead them on.

Now, there are three sorts of men in this world. Those who are instantly hostile to lesbianism, those who disregard it as something between women and of no consequence at all, unless it be the aperitif to the real thing, and those who are so excited by the thought that they will encourage it, even at their own expense.

Robin, that was his name, was in the third category I discovered, when I calmly declined his offer to make love but said that I would let him if I could have Rosamund first.

He trembled as I talked to him about it and gave his agreement to the plan without any hesitation. He was to bring her to me and leave her with me, but first he was to tell her what I wanted to do and then say she was to submit. When I had achieved what I wanted then, and only then, would I allow him to become my lover.

Actually, I had no intention of keeping my part of the bargain and calmly told him so. I had never been unfaithful to my husband with a man, and was not going to start now, but I did not say that. What I said was:

'What happens if I get fond of Rosamund? What happens if she responds so wholeheartedly that I feel I don't want to upset her by going to bed with her husband?'

He replied, 'I hope I would be sufficiently a gentleman not to insist.'

It was a tacit agreement between us, now he knew what I was, that the seduction of his wife was what he wanted. He would have liked the both, but it was Rosamund-the-fair in the arms of a lesbian woman that fascinated him. And for that he would agree to anything. I knew I had already won, because she was in awe of him. Not that he ever bullied her, but she always deferred to her husband. He was the dominant partner. .

I made one concession. I would tell him everything she said and did, right down to the last detail, whether I went to bed with him or not. And meanwhile, just for the hell of it, I resolved to make her jealous. I kissed her husband, under the mistletoe, for a whole minute full on the mouth, with my body pressed to his.

I was disappointed. Not for a moment did Rosamund show what she must have felt. But never mind, I thought, her turn will come. She was going to be so intimate with me that she would have no secret that I was not party to, no part of her slim, willowy figure unexplored by me, no emotion that I did not know about.

'You can call your soul your own,' I thought, 'but short of that, the rest is mine.' Was I being too confident? Perhaps.

Robin brought Rosamund round the next night, complete with a suitcase, to stay the night. I took her by the hand and led her to the bar, where I poured her out a large Pimms, laced with a tot of extra gin. I noticed her hand tremble as she took it.

'Look,' she said, 'let's just tell Robin we did whatever it is he wants and settle down to a nice evening in front of the fire.'

'Don't be silly' I said, 'that kiss I gave your husband under the mistletoe was to seal a promise. He promised me that I could have you, and I promised him that I was going to make love to you. I've wanted you ever since the first moment I saw you.'

I took her in my arms, one hand in her hair and the other on her firm little breast. Then I kissed her very gently. I could hardly believe I was doing it and that she was letting me. I slipped my tongue between her lips and explored her mouth. Then I pulled her down on the rug before the fire.

She said, 'You know I don't even like being touched by a woman,' as soon as I removed my mouth. I answered her by transferring my hand from her breast to her leg. Within a few minutes my fingers were probing her sex, which was as wide and wet as mine was. 'Little liar!' I said smiling at her.

'Yes, I know, I can't help it,' said Rosamund sullenly.

I slipped my hand inside her and right up without any difficulty. She was vibrating with sexual excitement.

'Well, we can't go on like this,' I replied, removing my fingers and licking them dry. 'You are coming to bed with me and you are going to do as you are told, just as Robin said. I don't care if you want to do it or not. Do you know you taste nice? I am going to taste more of you when I get you undressed.'

I pulled her to her feet and led her into the bedroom. Then I undressed her. Her small, firm breasts were pink-tipped and her pubic hair so light-coloured that at first I thought she was as hairless as a child. Then I saw there was quite a lot but most of it was damp with her sexual excitement, so her sex showed through. I could hardly wait to get my mouth on to it, but I thought I must not appear too impatient. I must take it slowly and make the girl eat her words – then I would have more to boast about to her husband. I realized this was going to be a battle of wills but I was going to win it; I was resolved on that. Rosamund was going to be conquered by another woman. She was going to like it so much that the next morning she was going to wonder why she had never done it before. I think if Rosamund had offered me a thousand pounds to let her off, I would have torn her cheque up in her face.

I pulled her on to the bed and slid on top of her, my nude body entwined with hers and we kissed mouth to mouth for a full ten minutes.

Then we lay and talked, my hand inside her, my thumb vibrating slowly on her clitoris.

I told her how beautiful she was and she told me how ashamed she felt at being so sexually aroused.

'You are going to be more ashamed in a minute,' I said 'I am going to kiss you between the legs and you are going to like it!'

To my surprise she put one arm around my neck

and twined her fingers in my hair. Then she kissed me.

'Don't let's go that far,' Rosamund said, with a tremble in her voice. 'It might not be very nice for you, even if I do like it.'

'It is the supreme compliment one woman can pay to another,' I replied, reaching for a pillow which I pulled under her bottom. She did not argue after that and I slid down to her pubic region which was, as I told her, in a most unladylike state.

'I don't know what Robin would think if he saw you now,' I told her, prising her thighs apart with my hands. Then I put my tongue inside her and she climaxed straight away. But she was not getting off that easy. I had only just started with her and my tongue soon found her clitoris and brought it into my mouth to be sucked like a sweet. She tasted nice, as I knew she would, like honey. As fast as I dried her she was wet again and she vibrated like a violin.

Suddenly she thrust both her hands into my hair, dragging it over my head, and my face was trapped firmly between her thighs. I could hardly breathe but I kept my tongue working on her then, without warning, she let go of my hair and surrendered to a long low climax – orgasm after orgasm – all in my mouth and moaning like the ghost of Hamlet's father.

As the last whimper died, after I had licked her clean and dried her with my thick brown hair, I slid up to kiss her just once on her mouth. Then I reached over the side of the bed and switched off the tape recorder. Later, Robin would hear it all, unbeknown to his wife, who was settling down to sleep naked in my arms.

'I don't think you'll ever be completely satisfied with a man again,' I said, 'once you've been licked out by another woman you never really forget it.'

She did not argue. She put her arms around me and returned my kiss. Just before she dropped off to sleep she said, 'I love you. It was heaven.'

I smiled to myself and put my face in her silky, blonde hair and took a deep breath. She smelt so feminine and she was all mine. All mine, by orders of her husband in the first place, but all mine in my own right now. I took one of her breasts in my hand and drifted off to sleep.

In the morning I did it to her again with similar results.

When her husband came for her he could see by the smirk on my face that his little wife had given satisfaction. An hour later he came back and, as I had promised, I told him everything and played the tape to him. His eyes were wide with excitement as he listened and to help him, I put my hand inside his trousers. He had a climax as he listened to his wife's cries with my hand hardly moving. I just held him, that was all, and then asked for her to be sent back to me in a week's time.

I suppose we made love half a dozen times like that, Rosamund and me, and then I dropped her without explanation. I was just tired of her and wanted to move to pastures new.

Her husband Robin, came round and begged me to have her back. 'All right,' I said, 'just once.'

And just once it was. She gave herself passionately to me and then I kissed her goodbye.

Poor Rosamund! But I could not go on. She was getting too intense. Too willing. She even let me smack her bottom with my hand, and came back and asked for more. So I gave her more, but it could not continue. I sent her back to her husband with orders to behave. I have no idea whether she did, but I expect so. The smacks were just love taps of course, nothing brutal. Her husband laughed when I told him.

Her last message was, 'Anytime you want me, just send for me.' She looked so pathetic I pushed her into a chair and quickly found her vagina with my questing fingers. Then I worked her to an orgasm as I kissed her goodbye. It was a good thing she was returning by car. I do not think she could have walked when I had finished with her bottom.

As she drove off I thought back to the distant, reserved girl she was when first I met her.

'She was as pure as snow,' I recited to myself, 'and like the snow, she drifted.'

A week later, my husband announced he was off to the United Kingdom for the Ministry of Defence to do some book-writing, in other words bringing a technical manual on a gunsight up to date.

Almost as soon as I realized I was to be a grass widow, Rosamund heard about it and rang me to say she would keep me company in the evenings, if I wanted her to do so.

'But I have decided to go to Austria for a holiday,' I said.

'Can I come with you?'

'But what will Robin say?' I replied. 'He'll be all alone.'

'Oh, he won't mind, he'll let me.'

I had enjoyed Rosamund. I can taste her fair fragrant skin as I write. She just got a bit too intense for my liking. But she would come in handy if I was going skiing in Austria. I like someone to fetch and carry, so I relented. She could come.

Robin rang the hotel and booked his wife in, and actually ordered a double-bedded room, not a twin-bedded one. He seemed genuinely pleased that I was going to take his wife away from him for a fortnight. Just for a moment, I wondered if he had a mistress, who was going to console him. But no, I think he genuinely wanted Rosamund to enjoy herself with me. He was like my husband, only more so. John never wanted to get rid of me, he just liked the stories. I sometimes used to tell him my tales of derring-do when he was actually inside me. This was when I wanted to produce the maximum effect.

Robin saw us off at the railway station. My husband had already flown off to Heathrow. Rosamund kissed her husband affectionately, and so did I. Robin said to me:

'Look after her, won't you,' and I replied: 'I will, and in more ways than one.'

We laughed and Robin said: 'I am so glad she is going with you. She always looks radiant after a session with you. And with a whole fortnight ahead, she will be in her seventh heaven.'

What a nice unselfish husband, I thought, as the train drew away.

We had a first-class carriage to ourselves. I took hold of Rosamund's hand and drew her to me.

'We are going to enjoy ourselves.' I said.

'Oh, yes!' Rosamund gazed at me with unconcealed admiration in her eyes, holding her mouth up to be kissed.

After a while we reached the snow line, and Rosamund, watching the falling snow flakes in the gathering darkness, declared, with childlike enthusiasm:

'It's like fairyland!'

We climbed higher and higher all night. One could almost hear the engine straining as it surged through the darkness of the snow-filled night. Rosamund and I cuddled up in a corner under a rug.

'I am so happy Jane. I love you.'

Yes, she was a bit intense, but with a fortnight ahead, her ready passion was going to save me a lot of routine courting.

They served breakfast on the train, with delicious hot coffee, and we arrived at our stop at 11 a.m. Waiting for us was the hotel bus, complete with snow chains, which drove us to our destination: a pretty little Austrian village, with a street of shops, in a wooded valley full of snow.

'Now this *is* fairyland!' I said to Rosamund. 'You were quite right.'

We checked in and were shown to our room on the top floor.'

'Would you rather have twin beds?' said the chambermaid, 'I can get it changed.'

'No, thank you,' I said. 'My friend has night-mares. She has just come out of hospital.'

'Always a ready fib to your lips,' my mother used to say, disparagingly.

After lunch, we went for a walk; looked at the little shops, hired our skis, and ski-sticks, bought our tickets for the ski-lifts, and then went to have cakes and chocolate in a little cafe as the sun went down with the suddenness characteristic of the High Tyrol.

After dark it was even more romantic, and as we walked back to the hotel the snow was falling silently: it decorated my brown hair and Rosa-mund's blonde hair like jewels from heaven.

'I hope poor Robin is not too lonely.' I remarked.

'I am not thinking about Robin now,' said Rosa-mund simply, 'I am thinking about you, and the fact that I am going to be in your arms all night.'

We had a table in the corner at dinner, and were able to observe the other guests.

There was a table with a typical Prussian family, grandfather, grandmother, son, daughter-in-law, and children. They clicked, bowed, kissed hands as each member of the family arrived. There were some young English couples and there were two girls, quite pretty, on holiday together. I wondered if they were like us – or were they on the hunt? They could have been a bit of both, of course.

After the evening meal we danced, taking care not to dance too close together, and I noticed the other couple danced together too. Luckily, women can always dance with each other without causing comment.

Rosamund said: 'I want to get closer to you than this.'

'Well you can't. People will talk.' I replied.

'Then let's go to bed. We can there.'

We disengaged, and wandered off to our room. Once inside I took her in my arms and kissed her, unzipping her evening dress as I did so. We were soon in bed, lying naked side by side, in supreme comfort in a centrally heated bedroom, with double-glazed windows and thick, drawn curtains.

I put my fingers on her vulva and stroked the fine, fair hair, which failed in any real way to conceal her genitals from the curious gaze.

'Your pubic hair is much thicker than mine,' said Rosamund, 'I have to disentangle it with my tongue before I can get inside you.'

'For a girl who once told me she did not even like being touched by a woman, you have come a long way,' I said. 'Had you ever been touched by a woman?'

'Yes,' replied Rosamund, 'by my mother's dressmaker in Paris. She was fat and fifty with a mass of dark hair in a bun, and a moustache like a man. She used to touch me everywhere at each fitting, and I hated it. Then when I was being measured for my apres-ski trousers, the ones I wore this afternoon, she touched my vagina quite deliberately. Embarrassing though it was, I said, 'Stop it, please,' but she took no notice of me, and I told her I would report her to my mother.

' "Madam will not believe you," she said. "Your mother knows me well, and will not accept the word of a 17-year-old girl against mine. Not even if you are her daughter.

' "But it will be as well if you didn't. If you don't, I will not charge for the apres-ski suit."

'I thought,' said Rosamund, 'that it would save Mother a hundred guineas or so. So I said:

' "Alright. I won't tell."

'At that the woman thrust her whole hand inside my pants and her fingers inside my vagina saying once again as she did so that she would not charge for the apres-ski suit. She brought me off, eventually by removing my pants and applying her mouth and moustache to my genitals. I could feel her moustache, all stiff and prickly on the inside of my vagina. Despite myself, it excited me, and I can remember grasping her bun in both hands, so it all came down, just as I climaxed.'

'Sounds to me as if you enjoyed it!' I replied.

'No, I didn't,' said Rosamund seriously. 'I hated it. The climax was purely physical. When Mother got the bill she noticed she hadn't been charged for the trouser suit, and I had to explain that it was a free gift because she had ordered so much.

' "Strange," said my mother, "The Hon. Maud's fat daughter was fitted out with just as much as you, and Maud was charged."

' "Well, perhaps it was because all the extra material needed for a fat girl costs more," I suggested lamely.

'I got away with it,' said Rosamund, opening her legs to me adoringly, 'but my face was scarlet. I don't know what mother thought I was blushing about.'

Telling this story had excited her, I noticed with my fingers, so I am not sure about her theory that she did not enjoy herself. She may well have been disgusted with herself afterwards, when she looked at the age and lack of beauty of the woman who had assaulted her, but I think she gave her little 17-year-old self to that Frenchwoman with complete abandon. That is why she clutched at the woman's bun and pulled it down, so she could get her hands in it as she climaxed. Rosamund was not kidding me and I doubt if she deceived the French dressmaker, whose moustached mouth would have told her all she needed to know, that this pure, fair-haired English schoolgirl had surrendered to her and enjoyed her first real French genital kiss from a matron of that land with true girlish abandon.

'I hated it, but I love it with you. You're different.'

I gathered Rosamund in my arms and, mounting her, proceeded to take her husband's place.

'Would you rather be in bed with Robin or a woman?' I asked.

'Oh, a woman every time if that woman is you, Jane,' said Rosamund putting her arms around me. I felt rather pleased. Here was a beautiful young married woman freely choosing to be petted by me, rather than by her husband, of whom she was very fond. It was quite an achievement and another illustration of the old proverb, that still waters run deep. I took her breast in my hand and put the nipple in my mouth and sucked it.

'Did the Frenchwoman do this to you?' I asked.

'Yes,' said Rosamund, 'she did everything. She

even showed me her vagina, which was a lot hairier than yours is and made me kiss it.'

'Mmm,' I thought, 'they had quite a party, those two, didn't they? My little innocent here almost qualifies for Shakespeare's "Me thinks she doth protest too much!" Or else the French dressmaker was a very experienced seductress. A bit of both I expect.'

Out loud I said: 'How you could bring yourself to do that to a fat, middle-aged Frenchwoman, I cannot think.'

'She made me.' replied Rosamund.

'Well you could have screamed!' I asserted.

'Yes, I suppose I could have done.' She put her tongue in my mouth, as I released her breast, with its nipple standing erect now, and kissed her. We had the bedroom lights full on, and were enjoying each other.

We skied, danced and made love all through that delightful fortnight, and I began to wonder how I could have nearly paid Rosamund off. But the fact remained that she was very clinging and so very dependent. Perhaps it was because, although I loved her – and how could anyone fail to love her? – I was not *in love* with her. Also, when I fell in love with a girl, I would want her all to myself and not have to share her with a man.

One evening we went out with two young Austrians. They were ski instructors who, with great determination, tried to seduce us. We let them kiss us and Rosamund let her boy pet her, I noticed disapprovingly, but we would not go to bed with them.

'Why not?' They said, 'We are good.'

'So are we, and that's why we won't. We have both got husbands, and we are faithful wives.'

They looked hurt and puzzled, but it was no use them arguing. We were adamant. But they took it with fairly good grace. We had all had a pleasant evening, and we thanked them for escorting us. Robin would never have forgiven me if I had let his little pet lamb commit adultery, and I think she might have done so, if I had not been there.

The fortnight passed swiftly, too swiftly really because it was great fun. I löved the sun and the clear air and the white snow, together with the healthy exercise. We slept like logs, sometimes we were so tired we just cuddled and did not make love until the morning.

Robin was very pleased to see her back, and to hear my detailed account of our adventures. His regiment moved to Gibraltar soon after that, and Rosamund kissed me a tearful goodbye in the ladies' cloakroom at the airport. We could never have kissed, as we wanted to kiss, out in the open.

I have had many girls since her, but I have never quite forgotten that particular conquest. And conquest it was. I needed her husband's help just to get into position, but the actual conquest and subjugation was my work, and mine alone. I do not suppose it did her any harm. Or Robin.

6

Chapter 6

John was sent to an establishment run by the Royal Corps of Signals for a six months' course in a new battlefield technique of rapid communications. The army had come a long way from the days when the only method of getting a message through was by that appalling example of British technology, the field telephone. I can remember my father telling me that a signal from the front line, which started out as:

'The enemy is advancing on both flanks, send reinforcements,'

arrived as:

'The enemy is dancing on wet planks, send three and fourpence.' I can well believe it. The soldiers used to call them 'Honkle-yang-yangs,' because that is what everything sounded like when one applied one's ear to the hole provided for the purpose.

The course was, naturally, held miles away from where we lived. The Services specialize in dividing up families whenever possible, as often as possible. I reconciled myself to being a grass widow, with

the occasional weekend of sex and laughter when
John returned to the regiment. It was not the first
time we had been apart and it would not be the
last. I found myself wondering if Emma had
arranged the posting. I can remember her saying
once: 'I like a girl to be really sex-starved when I
get her. An army wife who is terribly faithful, but
has not seen her husband for months is my ideal
bedmate.'

That was going to be my situation soon, and
Emma would be round to see me I supposed. Well,
she was very good at it, as Sue and I both knew to
our mutual pleasure. It was a pity I did not still
have Sue. I was never sex-starved with little Sue in
the house, even if John was away. My present girl
was a German, pretty and well upholstered, but I
had not got round to her yet. Lisa was her name
and she kept the place so clean and well organized
there was never much for me to do.

It was about a fortnight before Emma, very much
the Colonel's wife, came round to see if I was all
right, and it did not take her very long to get me
into bed. I was just about ready for it and gave
into her easily, as her tongue sought that currently
neglected part of me, that source of my pleasure
John used to stimulate so easily. I may be a lesbian,
but with John I could be the very paragon of
normality, that is if you exclude the thoughts and
fantasies that pre-occupied me whenever I was near
to orgasm. Happily, there are no thought police in
the army provost, not yet anyway. Perhaps even
that will come, if Soviet espionage techniques get

any more sophisticated. I will have to watch out then, they will get me straight away.

'You won't be lonely while your husband is away,' said Emma, 'I intend to take his place in the marriage bed from time to time.'

I thanked her with the necessary look of gratitude and humility on my face. Emma was not my type really, though she was very good at it. I do not much like grey hair, though hers was very soft and shiny. But I mostly did not like her proprietary air. Anyone would think she owned me just because she was the Officer Commanding's wife. However, none of this was imparted by anything I said. Emma could be a very dangerous woman if crossed. It was far better for her to think I liked her. I opened my mouth as she kissed me, and let her have her way. She liked having her way and especially with the wife of one of her husband's officers. Emma was the one woman I had never told John about, the one exception to my rule of confessing everything. To start with, I did not want him to think he had got promoted by the efforts of his wife and, secondly, I do not really think the colonel's wife had much to do with it. John was a first-class soldier and you just cannot keep a good man down. But I will tell him one day when we are out of the army perhaps – but not now.

My husband's course was being held in a small town with a name which begins with Bad. There was not enough accommodation for all the officers and other ranks attending, so John was billeted out in a boarding house run by an ex-patriot English woman called Loveday, who seemed to have eaten her husband, if she had ever had one. She was startlingly good-looking, to my husband's delight because, faithful or not, it is nice to have someone pleasant to look at. The little hotel was totally devoid of staff, John discovered, when he found that Loveday was not only in the kitchen, but was waitress, receptionist and housemaid. Of course, gallantly he helped her, he was always kind.

'When the army sent you all here I was closing down at the end of the season,' said Loveday. 'I will get some staff tomorrow. But thanks for helping me.'

Loveday was in her thirties, with very dark, shoulder-length hair, with an odd strand of grey. She was tall for a woman, and her blue eyes were in contrast to her colouring. Her figure was full and promising. John told me he was going to need all his powers of fidelity if he was to withstand this siege. Had I been there I would have been instantly jealous. She was just the sort of woman that makes my hackles stand on end when she is after my man, and she was going to be after my man, as John soon discovered.

As the course progressed, John got to know Loveday quite well. He took her to a cinema once and quite often they would dine alone in one of the many little eating places in the villages around.

She had, indeed, been married. She had divorced her husband, a stockbroker, for running off with the teenaged daughter of his best friend. That was some ten years ago and she did not intend to repeat the experiment. Once bitten, twice shy, as she put it.

She asked John about me and he showed her his set of photographs of his wife in various stages of dress and undress. She had already noticed the routine framed photograph of me in the room which she had provided for him. It was, of course, the usual engagement photograph, taken by a fashionable London photographer.

'Your wife's very lovely,' she remarked. 'You must miss her a lot.'

'Yes, I do,' said my husband 'but one has to expect separations in this job. It is all the nicer when one gets back. It is one long honeymoon really. You never get time to be bored with each other. That is why there are less divorces in the Services than outside.'

'Is she faithful?' said Loveday. 'She has a look in her eye that reminds me of a girl I knew once. And she wasn't faithful! Every time her husband turned his back she was into bed with the first man she could find.'

John flushed scarlet.

'Oh, yes, Jane's faithful. So am I. We both trust each other.'

'You may be right,' said Loveday, mischievously. 'But I would watch her just the same. She has a look in her eye. I am a woman and I know.'

Loveday was looking at a photograph of me in my underclothes, powdering my face at my dressing table.

'Who took this?' she asked.

'I took it. We were just going off to the General's annual ball at Divisional Headquarters.'

'It might have been another man, might it not?

111

I'll tell you what. I bet you anything you like, your wife strays occasionally. All women do.'

She was trying to make my husband jealous and the reason was quite obvious. She was setting her cap at him. However, it was not working. John got to his feet and suggested it was time to return, as the course was starting an hour early tomorrow.

'Aren't you going to kiss me goodnight?'

Loveday got to her feet too and they kissed in the moonlight of the hotel garden by John's car.

'I am sorry I said that about Jane, I expect she's a super girl. I was just trying to be provocative. I'll tell you what, get Jane down here for a week and I won't charge anything for her board and lodging. I'd like to meet her. I have a feeling we would get on.' Loveday was trying to repair the damage.

'Thank you,' John replied, 'I'll see what she says when I ring her tonight.'

My husband told me afterwards that there was something about Loveday and her off-beat conversation that excited him. He was, he said, as hard as a ram as he kissed her, and she knew it.

'I'd love you to be unfaithful to your wife with me,' said Loveday. 'Then when I meet her I can look in her eyes and think about it. I'd like that.'

She put her hand down and touched the bulge in my husband's dress trousers.

'You could do it easily. Jane's a long way away, perhaps in the arms of another man, and you want me, don't you?'

'I am sure she's not in the arms of another man and, of course I want you, but I don't think it would be very wise.'

John can be stuffy when he wants to be.

As they drove back, there was an awkward silence between them. The battle was not over yet. This was just a preliminary skirmish.

When my husband rang me that night I sensed something was on his mind and readily agreed to his plan for me to come down for a week during the break, which was equivalent to half-term. I told him to thank his landlady for her generous offer, which I accepted with pleasure.

'What does she look like?' I asked.

'She's pretty. I think you'll like her.'

'Is she *my* type?'

'I don't know,' my husband said, 'she could be, but that's not the sort of thing you can ask a woman at first acquaintance.'

We laughed. I have a sort of telepathy with John. He was on to something but I was not quite sure what. 'I'd better go down and find out!' I thought. 'Send me her photograph,' I said. 'Then I will know what to expect. How old is she?'

'A bit older than you, I think. She's in her thirties.'

'Have you kissed her?' I asked.

My husband is not a very good liar. I could feel his confusion at the end of the line.

'Well, yes,' he replied. 'Just once. It was just a peck.'

'Did you enjoy it?' I asked, to tease him.

'You know me darling. I am never unfaithful. I only want you.' Yes, I did know, I have always been sure of John, but I was not sure of this other woman. I had to gird my loins for battle, like they did in the olden days, I mused. 'Oh well, life is never dull for long, not in the army.'

I had three weeks to wait and then I intended to motor down to see my husband. Three weeks for Loveday to amuse herself with John, or vice versa. He sent me a snap shot he had taken, and it confirmed my fears. She was very lovely.

However, I need not have worried. John went very near the brink and certainly amused himself, but he was faithful. They did have oral sex though. It was as far as he would go.

It happened when she came to his room one morning and got into bed with him. They kissed, and Loveday quite plainly made herself available. But John was adamant. He let her put his penis in her mouth and he told me, afterwards, he enjoyed it very much, but he said 'No' to full sex. 'Jane and I are never unfaithful to each other. Kissing yes, but not all the way, no matter how much we want to, was what we agreed when we married.'

'I bet you anything Jane cheats on that one,' said Loveday, moving her mouth from John's penis for a second.

John gathered up her hair in his hand prior to his climax. He always liked to keep the girl's mouth there until he was through. He need not have worried, Loveday had no intention of removing her mouth until he had finished. She was trying very hard to capture John. And she captured all of my husband's sperm, even if the man himself eluded her.

They did that quite frequently during the next couple of weeks and Loveday obviously hoped he would weaken, but he did not. He quite liked oral sex and if she was willing to provide it, free of charge, why not?

Once when she was doing it, quite skilfully John said, she took her mouth away from the knob for a moment and remarked:

'I hope Jane likes me.'

'I am sure she will like you,' replied my husband, pressing her head down to his loins again.

'She'd better not like me *too* much,' Loveday said, 'I have lesbian inclinations.'

John started. He grew even harder. She removed her mouth again and remarked, 'And I won't need your help. I'll seduce her all by myself, and in the morning she will wonder why she did it.'

Loveday replaced her mouth to receive, at that instant, my husband's ejaculation. Until that moment she had not realized how her words had excited him. He held her head down until he was spent and doubtless she knew then that she was in a different ball game. A very different game. If she could not have the man, then there was always the wife. She would take her from him and make him so jealous he would want both of them. That would kill two birds with one stone.

'Will you be angry if I do?' asked Loveday. 'I won't hurt her. Not unless you want me to,' she added slyly, looking at the man out of the corner of her eye. 'I'll beat her if you want me to.'

'I don't want her to be beaten. But I should not be angry if you made love to her. That is, if she wants you to. I don't call sex between women infidelity. In fact, it rather excites me.'

'So I noticed,' said Loveday turning her mouth down. 'You nearly drowned me. And I'll nearly drown Jane when I get hold of her. You see. It will be a sweet revenge.'

John was erect again and pulled Loveday's head down.

'I'll take it out on Jane,' she said, laughing. 'You are making a rod for her back. I shall punish her for what you have done.'

'We'll think about that later,' my husband replied, replacing his steaming knob where it had rested so comfortably just before. 'Go on till I've finished, and you can do what you like with Jane.'

'I will, don't you worry!' said Loveday viciously. 'What will happen will be between Jane and me, and there will be no one there to help her. But she'll love it. I'm the world's expert.'

'Modesty, thy name is Loveday,' I thought, when John told me this story a lot later.

John was so excited by this remark that he went down on Loveday for the first time. She opened her legs willingly for him saying:

'I shall make Jane do this and I won't wash first. I'll make her do the washing with her tongue and go on until I am quite clean.'

How John had the self-control not to throw himself on Loveday and rape her there and then, I shall never know. They were both so excited about me, a girl one of them had never seen, except in a photograph, that they both climaxed together, Loveday having turned end for end.

My husband told me he went to sleep in the morning lecture and I do not wonder. If I had known what was going on I would have been seriously alarmed by my husband planning the seduction of his wife with a beautiful divorcee. Up to now in his marriage, he had merely listened, with eyes square with interest, to the lurid accounts of his dear wife's indiscretions. He was now about to take a more active role, arranging with another woman the actual details of his wife's seduction. And Loveday was relishing her part in the proposed adventure. In a way she was making the man unfaithful, without him actually having full sex with her, which she would have liked. Loveday wanted it all, but if she could not get all, she would settle for Jane. She told me later her mouth watered at the thought of having the wife as a possible substitute. 'I had already fallen in love with your photograph and I couldn't wait to get my hands on you.'

First the wife, then her husband, that was Loveday's full plan. She was going to ask me to let her have John, and then go all the way with him, with me watching. 'I'll see about that.' I thought, when I was told the prospects.

John's course was proceeding normally but, somehow, I do not think he was concentrating very much. He would have to do a lot of last minute revision if the examination at the end of the course was not to reveal his lack of attention. Happily my husband is clever, and he knew quite a lot about what he was being told already. He was a professional soldier to his finger tips, and did not need half the course on which he was sent by the army. Some of his friends had to work very hard to pass their examinations, but John took examinations for a pastime.

'I've always been able to put down on paper what little I know,' he once told me, 'and that just gets me a pass mark.' Very self-effacing, is my soldier, but I think he is above average, and I would not be surprised if he reaches Brigadier or beyond. That is if he does not slip up over some enthusiastic female like Loveday. The Ministry of Defence is rather old-fashioned about that sort of thing – if it ever comes to official notice.

'You can do all sorts of things in the army,' my father once said, 'but you must never be found out. That is the real crime.'

If the army ever found out what I had been up to, it would not have helped my husband's career. Happily, only Emma knew, and she would not tell. I often wondered if the Colonel knew about his wife? Somehow, I did not think so. He was a rather conservative man, and I could not see him approving. But you never know, perhaps he did know about it.

Somewhere perhaps there is a hidebound, regimental book-man with enough sexual imagination to understand the affairs of women with each other. Perhaps. . . . But I think Emma was just a rather vicious, senior wife, using her husband's rank, unbeknown to him, to bring younger women to heel. Heaven only knows how many young wives submitted to her caresses to further their husband's careers. And some of them unlike me, would have hated every minute of the ordeal. I enjoyed it, but then I would, would I not?

I tried very hard to make Emma believe I was reluctant, but the outward and visible signs must have told her otherwise, and she had had a lot of experience of women. She knew which were the reluctant ones and which were having a ball. Frankly, I think she preferred the former and if she could get some shrinking girl, with an inadequate soldier husband to accede to her wishes, she never hesitated to take advantage of her. She was a menace, if only to the efficiency of the regiment, though, to be honest, I never saw anyone promoted who ought not to have been, so I think Emma took the wife and did not keep the promises she made to them. John's promotion meant nothing. I could not see him failing to be promoted. I could have told her to chase herself if I had wanted to. I like being seduced by an older woman, or seeming to be seduced. I am only butch when I want to be. I wonder if I ought to be in the *Guinness Book of Records* as the best example of the sexually versatile woman? I must ask John. He is very proud of me, I know, but I think he would draw the line at that.

In due course, others got wind of John's friendship with Loveday and one of the army wives told me what was going on. She had heard from her husband that John was having an affair with a most attractive and unattached woman who was a little older than he was, but I should watch it just the same, she said. It was meant kindly and I accepted it as such. But, on the surface I laughed it off. Our men often flirted with other women, when they were away. All men did. They would not be men if they did not. But I was making plans just the same. I had my own methods and my own weapons.

Meanwhile, John was enjoying the company of Loveday. She was a well-educated woman, having read the humanities at Oxford, and with two good second-class degrees, she was above average for intelligent and lively conversation of the sort men seem to like. She was certainly well out of my class for repartee and witticisms and that, coupled with her striking colouring – straight very dark hair and blue eyes – made her a woman not to be overlooked, especially when she was making a dead set at my husband.

Loveday even knew how to fish. She could cast a fly in any company and she and John would spend evening after evening, after dinner, fishing the waters of a wooded lake a mile or two from the hotel. And she was not too soft-hearted to land the trout she caught.

The only time I ever went fly-fishing was when someone lent my father a mile of a trout stream in Devon. I fished all summer and only caught one. Having wept over it, I rushed home to have it cooked for supper. It did not taste all that wonderful. It was a rather small, brown trout, and I can remember thinking that I would have rather had bread and butter and let the poor little thing swim on in that bright, tumbling stream, with its mossy rocks.

But Loveday landed them by the dozen, and they tasted like lake trout should, firm and delicate, and pink-fleshed. She served them to her guests in her hotel, and they were well appreciated. There was a special knack required to catch the trout in that particular lake. On the very first evening they tried every fly they had without success, so Loveday went to the local tackle shop and discovered that there was only one fly that attracted the fish in that particular lake. After that, the fishing improved, and so did their liking for each other. John was still in love with me, and our relationship was never in danger, but as a jealous woman, and in retrospect, the affair had gone further than I would have wanted it to. They kissed, flirted, had oral sex, at which Loveday was so good, John said, but they stopped short of the real thing. John never committed adultery he said, and I believed him. He deliberately set his face against it, as his sop to Cerberus, the salve to his conscience, and it needed one.

I had often said to my husband:

'When you are away I don't expect you not to enjoy the company of other women, if you want to, that is. I trust you completely.'

It was that last sentence that he remembered, and in love with his wife as he was, Loveday was fighting a hopeless battle. However, she thought she was doing rather well. She had noticed how remarks she made about me, sharp and wounding remarks at times, seemed to excite John. She enjoyed exciting men she found attractive, and so she persevered.

'Has Jane ever had another woman in bed with her? A lesbian woman, I mean.'

'I don't think so,' said John, and I hope he said his prayers that night. 'She may have had a crush

121

on another schoolgirl when she was in her teens. You had better ask her.'

'I will,' said Loveday, 'I will. I shall ask her quite a lot of things and I can usually extract the answers when I want to. I'll find out if she has ever been unfaithful to you. And you remember what I said, don't you? I think she has.'

That night Loveday let herself into John's room. She had a pass-key of course, but my husband could have locked the door if he had wanted to. He chose not to and I do not blame him. She was in a black, nylon nightdress with her hair loose and flowing, and her mind set on some sort of sexual adventure.

John pulled back the sheets and let her in. She slid on top of him, seductively, and said:

'How far do you want me to go with Jane?'

'That's up to you,' said my brave and supportive husband, 'That's up to you and Jane.'

'Jane won't have much say in it. I have already made up my mind about that. All I want is a promise from you, and you must keep it, not to come to her rescue. You must abandon her to me, and no matter what you hear, keep out of the room.'

Loveday was moving suggestively on John, who was physically excited, not only by her presence – and what man would not have been – but by what she had said to him.

'Your young wife and I are going to get to know each other very well. Tell me, and you needn't if you don't want to, because I shall find out for myself, but how long is her clitoris?'

'I think you had better find out for yourself. Honestly Loveday, the things you ask!'

As I have remarked earlier, my husband can suddenly, at the most unexpected times, be overcome with what can only be described as army stuffiness – schoolboy-like embarrassment would possibly be a more appropriate phrase.

Loveday was quite equal to him. Nothing put her off her balance. Taking John's penis in her hand and looking at it appreciatively, she said: 'I shall find out, don't you worry. Jane will show me.'

She calmly trailed her loose, soft hair over his penis for a few moments and then, wrapping it up like a parcel in her hair, addressed herself to the important end.

'Does Jane do this to you?'

'Yes,' said John, shortly.

'But not as well as I do, I bet. We'll have a competition one day, Jane and I. But first we'll have one with each other. I am quite looking forward to laying your wife you know.'

Loveday's words excited my husband. She could see they did and she enjoyed doing it. The lady was not a true lesbian, she was like me, completely bi-sexual. She did everything to induce John to go all the way with her, but he resisted. Oral sex was as far as he would venture. I am glad he was strong because she would have boasted about it to me. As it was, all she could admit to was her hair being a sodden mess, which had to be washed that very night, or she would never have got a comb through it in the morning. John never does things by halves, and when she wrapped her long hair round his erect penis, she did it at her mortal peril, if that is not too dramatic a description for the expenditure of the contents of a small bottle of fairly expensive shampoo.

And all the time this was happening, I was lying alone in bed at home. I could have rung Emma I suppose, but I was on to something new and could not wait to meet Loveday.

The days dragged on. I packed most of my things in preparation for a long stay. I was not going to come home and leave John with that girl. Even a good and loyal husband has his limitations and if, one day, John had a bit too much to drink he might go too far. Alcohol has that effect on some men, I have noticed. Some want to fight, some want to sleep, and some get amorous. John was one of the latter.

Just before I was due to leave, one of the army wives came to see me. She was very young, about 19, and while her husband was away, she was getting anonymous telephone calls from a man. Now, I am liberal about most sexual deviations, but obscene telephone calls to women make me see red. They are so stupid for one thing, and so frightening for another, especially if you are a nervous sort of girl. June, the 19-year-old, was that sort. She was pretty, demure, fair-haired and was near to tears as she told me about it.

Apparently the man rang up every afternoon and most evenings. If she put the phone down it rang again and the voice would say: 'Now that was silly, wasn't it?'

Then the voice would go on as if nothing had happened.

I thought of going to the Military Police, but that might lead to the girl giving evidence in court.

'I'll tell you what,' I said, 'I'll be there when he rings you this afternoon. Leave it to me.'

The phone rang at 2 o'clock sharp and as June went to one phone, I picked up the extension and listened.

'How are you, June?' the voice said. 'I can see you from my window.' There was a block of flats opposite. The voice was English, but there was some sort of accent.

'I want you to masturbate while I talk to you. I am masturbating, and I am looking at you as I am doing it. Do you know what I would like to do to you?'

June, the little cuckoo, started to cry, audibly.

'That's right,' said the voice. 'Cry! You'll cry all right when you get this up you. Especially if I take you from behind. That's the way I usually do it, and it will hurt you.'

'Please don't ring me up anymore,' said June, between sobs. 'It frightens me.'

'You are right to be frightened,' said the voice, with added menace. 'And I like frightening you. My cock is twice as big since you started to cry. When I come over I'll make you cry even more. Tell me, do you like screwing?'

In my most unladylike voice I shouted, 'I'd like to screw the balls of a silly bastard like you to the wall with a six inch nail and a Glasgow screwdriver!'

Abruptly the phone went dead, and he never rang again. I hope he thought it was his victim, and that the worm had turned. The moral of all this is never to cry when you get an obscene telephone call. It only encourages them.

I sat and cuddled June on the sofa after that. She was very pretty, and I could have gone further, but I thought she had gone through enough. I did, however, kiss her on the cheek just once, and put her on my reserve list in case I was ever short.

'I'll never forget what you have done to help me.' she said.

'Well, next time do it yourself. You know the words now!' I said, sympathetically. 'Men always go for a frightened girl, but they can't stand a strident virago.'

7

Chapter 7

I left home early that morning; Lisa was half asleep as she helped me with my bags and promised to keep an eye on the house. We had to pay her while I was away, so I gave her a long list of spring cleaning to do. She said she hoped I would find my husband well, and I kissed her on the forehead, in a sort of maternal way, to say goodbye. Her hair, touselled and fresh from bed, smelt sweet and I can remember thinking, 'If I hadn't had so much on my mind I'd have taken a tumble with Lisa. I've not had a German girl since Claire. I must be slipping!'

The early morning air was nice and fresh as I drove down the autobahn to the south. I stopped for breakfast at about 7 o'clock for hot chocolate and fresh bread and butter. I do not normally bother about breakfast, but I enjoyed that breakfast. Mine host was still abed, after a hard night pouring beer down the throats of his thirsty customers I expect, so I was served by the cook

himself, fresh from baking the bread. I told him I
thought it was delicious.

'Ah,' he said, 'the fresh air and fresh new bread
go well together. You must get up early more often,
mein frau.' His schoolgirl daughter came to clear
away and I can remember thinking that many of
the German girls, especially the very young ones,
took a lot of beating for beauty. I gave her a tip
and she thanked me so prettily I wished I had
given her more. But I had to be careful with money.
If I intended to run two homes for a bit, unless I
could organize one end free, I would have to budget
to the last mark. My mother says that John and I
are just spendthrifts. When father was in the army
his pay was only four and six pence a day, or
something ridiculously small like that. 'Now, look
at the money servicemen are paid,' she would say.
I presume we are paid adequately, but it is carefully
calculated for each family to stay put and not motor
all over the place, running two homes.

My mind turned to the journey ahead. I was not
leaving John alone with that woman any longer.
'That woman' is, of course, the last retort of the
defeated party and I was not defeated yet, not by
a long chalk, I thought to myself. I will re-phrase
my deliberations, I was not going to leave my
husband alone with that girl any longer.

I like driving. You can think when driving, as
long as it is a straight run, as this one was. I had
left home looking as feminine as it was possible to
look, my hair freshly washed and my Sunday best
hat on the seat beside me. Jane was going to war
and the weapons were of her own choosing.

John had given me a good hand-drawn map to follow, and I arrived sharp at 10 o'clock, or 1000 hours, as the soldiers call it. I insisted on staying a civilian, even if I *had* married the army. And sometimes with the rules and regulations that beset you at every turn, you did feel you had married the army and not the individual boy with whom you had happened to have fallen in love.

Loveday met me on the doorstep. She had been waiting for this moment and we eyed each other like the two felines we really were, despite the smiles and the warm handshakes.

'John has told me so much about you.'

'Yes, I bet he has,' was the thought that went through my mind, but openly I said:

'Yes, and he has told me about you, and that you are the kindest landlady he has ever had.'

Loveday was looking ravishing. I could quite see what John saw in her. She was striking and beautiful, with a lot going for her. But so had I, and as that great American, John Paul Jones declared, I had not yet begun to fight.

After coffee and croissants, hot from the oven, Loveday took me out in the car. John was away on duty, of course.

'Would you like to drive down and see the lake, where we catch all those trout your husband has told you about?' she said.

'Yes, I would. He says you are a super fly fisherman, or fishergirl, rather. I have only caught one trout in my whole life, and when I'd caught it I wished I hadn't. Poor little thing.'

Loveday laughed. 'I'll teach you,' she said.

'I bet you will. I expect you would like to teach me lots of things if you get half a chance,' I thought.

We drove to the edge of the lake and my hostess produced, as if from nowhere, two glasses and a bottle of cold champagne. There was a little fridge in the back of the front seat, I discovered. 'Loveday is taking a lot of trouble with me,' I thought. 'But why not, I'm worth it.' My morale was high. I always know when I am going to win.

I looked at the calm waters of the lake, blue as the sky above and with the last whisps of the morning mist clearing with the warmth of the sun. Occasionally a fish rose to a fly and the widening circles of the rise slowly spanned out to meet other widening circles from another fishy meal. I could have sat watching it for ever. So this was where John and Loveday spent their evenings, catching fish and kissing between each cast, I expect. Loveday took my hand in hers. 'We are going to be friends.' she said. 'I am so glad you accepted my invitation. I have been dying to meet you.'

I smiled at her. She looked so lovely. I found myself gazing at her soft, shining hair and thinking: 'John will have had his hands in that.'

Loveday poured out some more champagne; I was beginning to enjoy myself. This was civilized campaigning, of the kind I liked. In a funny sort of way, I was beginning to like my hostess. We were two of the same sort, I suppose, even if we did eye each other warily as we talked.

'I do think you live in a nice neck of the woods,' I said. 'I could sit here for ever.'

'So could I,' replied Loveday, 'we'll come back

tomorrow if you like. We must all go fishing, too, one evening.'

We finished our champagne and drove back leisurely. It was a country road and we were unlikely to meet any police with breathalizers. Not that we had drunk too much. German sparkling wine, which our champagne really was, is very light and, although the French may not think so, every bit as good as the original product.

The hotel was buzzing by the time we returned. Loveday had the staff well trained and everything was done for her when she was away, without the necessity of her supervision, I noticed. I was shown to my room, a new double room to which my husband's things had only been moved that morning. I decided to re-new my make-up and changed my dress for a flowery summer frock. I looked at myself in the full length mirror. I was really very pretty I concluded, and it was not just vanity, all good-looking women know when they are at their best. My mother used to warn me against vanity as the besetting sin, to absolutely no avail. Her little daughter always knew she was attractive and no mother could persuade her otherwise. My hair was an inch or two longer than usual. John liked it like that, and we had been apart for quite a while. I felt my heart beating. I was very much in love and I had a husband in a million. And I was going to keep him.

I sat down by the dressing table as there was a soft tap on the door.

'Come in,' I said. Loveday entered to ask me if I had everything I wanted.

'Yes, thank you,' I replied, continuing to brush out my hair.

'Shall I do it for you?' asked Loveday, taking the brush from my hand as she said it. I like having my hair brushed.

Loveday said she loved that photograph of me at my dressing table that John had showed her.

'You mean the one in bra and pants.' I said, smiling.

'Yes, and he showed me the one without any bra and pants.'

'Oh, John is awful. That was meant to be private!' I replied, as she smoothed my hair down with her hand.

'He's very proud of his wife,' said Loveday 'and I don't blame him. She is every bit as pretty as the nicest photograph.'

'What time's lunch?' I asked, thinking things had gone far enough for the moment.

'There is a reception for you this evening at 6 o'clock, and lunch is a moveable feast. You can have it when you like,' was the reply. She bent down and kissed the top of my head, to my surprise, and said:

'I bet you are dying to see your husband.'

'Yes, I am,' I laughed, 'and I am sure he is thinking about me just at this moment. I am telepathic you know. I can always feel when he is thinking about me.'

We went down to lunch, which was preceded by a glass of sherry. Loveday said that everything I had while I was there, was to be on the house. I was her personal guest. It was very kind of her, but I knew there must be a motive.

After luncheon I offered to help my hostess, but all she said was:

'That's very sweet of you Jane, but I am going to do my accounts. If I were you, I should go up and have a little rest. If I know men, you are going to have a sleepless night!'

Despite my self-assurance, which I had put on like the armour of righteousness, I found myself blushing. Loveday smiled at me, amused at my confusion. If this were a race, she was just slightly in the lead now.

'Well, what man would spend the night *sleeping* with anyone as lovely as you in bed! Forgive me,' she said, 'if I have embarrassed you, I was only teasing.'

I tried to look nonchalant and opened my bag to sort out my door key. Loveday reached over and found it for me.

That afternoon seemed to be of an interminable length, but eventually the sound of a Range Rover brought me to the window and there was John. I raced downstairs and into his arms.

'Oh, I have missed you darling,' were his first words, and mine too. Loveday was watching as we embraced. Her eyes were hard.

We had tea on the verandah and as married couples, who are close to each other do, we talked ourselves out.

The reception was fun and it was kind of Loveday to arrange it. There were three of John's brother officers and one of their wives, down like me for a stay. They were billeted in the next hotel, and there were a number of locals as well as the other hotel guests. The drink was again champagne, made from local grapes, I was told. It was certainly very good and it began to have an effect on me. I put my glass down because I did not want to fall asleep as John was making love to me. I found myself thinking about bed and bedtime.

Eventually it all came to an end and John took me by the hand to lead me upstairs. Once inside the room, John took me in his arms and kissed me. There was a tap at the door.

'Come in,' said John, continuing to hold me in his arms. I could feel his penis hard against my leg. Loveday let herself in and, without a word to either of us, wrapped herself around me like some sort of clinging plant. Even then she seemed still to have one hand free to turn my face to hers, so that she could kiss me on the mouth. If anything, John got harder, and I was held firmly in place in the arms of both of them. After a few minutes Loveday said to John:

'Let me come to bed with you, and Jane will be much better value.' She turned me round so I was facing her, with my back to John.

'Just let me take charge of her and you won't know your wife. Go downstairs and pour yourself out a drink, and leave me with her for just 10 minutes. Here's the keys. I am going to instill a little discipline in your loving wife before we start.'

John went towards the door leaving me in Loveday's arms. I felt betrayed somehow.

'On second thoughts, make it half an hour. She

will be all ready for you then.' The door shut behind him, and we were alone.

'Now, Jane, we are going to get to know each other. And you, my pet, are going to do exactly as you are told. As you are told by *me*, not John. Your husband promised me a night with you when we were making love to each other last night. Oh, we didn't go all the way! He was faithful to you. He always is. But we went right up to the brink. Within a fraction of an inch. And we talked about you all the time.'

Loveday kissed me, holding me fiercely in her arms. She was taller than me and I kissed up to her and returned her affection, if it was affection I was returning. It was more like lust, I remember thinking, than affection. Well, if this is what John wanted I had better play ball. I do not much like a man watching while I am having sex with a girl, but I found myself concluding that this was different. It would be a woman watching a man making love to me. That might give it extra zest. I did not mind. And Loveday was pretty. Her tongue was in my mouth now and her hand pulled down the zip at the back of my evening dress. Soon I was standing nude before her with my hair loosened round my shoulders.

'This is like being in on the honeymoon,' declared Loveday. 'And I am going to see that the blushing bride does her duty by her man.' She took me in her arms again. There is something rather sensuous about being nude in the arms of another girl who is still fully dressed. Loveday's evening dress was made of silk and was cool to my naked body as she kissed me, with her fingers toying with my pubic hair.

After a few minutes she released me and took me to the bathroom. I suddenly realized that I was meant to sit down on the seat with her watching. She pushed me down and bent over and kissed me again. She put one hand between my legs. Her fingers probed insistently.

'No,' I said.

'You'll stay there, then, till you do.' replied Loveday, firmly, covering my vagina with her whole hand. Bowing to the inevitable I did what she told me. My face was crimson with embarrass-ment. Loveday just continued to kiss me as if nothing was happening between my legs, nothing at all.

When she was washing her hand afterwards, Loveday said, looking me straight in the face:

'You were lovely and hot. I suppose it was because you were thinking about John all day. You were, weren't you?' Then she dabbed me dry between my legs with the same towel, kissing me again as she did so.

'Come to bed,' she said, 'I am going to get you ready for your husband.' She led me to the bed and pushed me down on to it. Then standing above me, at the side of the bed, she undressed swiftly.

'There,' she said, as the last vestige of her under-clothes slid to the floor. 'This is what John gets hard over – this.' She put one leg across my face and put her wide open, hairy sex on to my mouth.

'This is what your husband has got excited about, night after night for months. He has touched it, licked it, put the tip of his penis against it, he has wanted it desperately, but he has always been faithful to you. And I bet you haven't been faithful to him. As I was fingering your vagina just now, I was thinking that you had probably had another man up you not too long ago. It felt used somehow, your vagina did.'

Loveday climaxed at that moment and filled my mouth with her love juices. I felt her shuddering as the wave of unbridled pleasure swept over her.

She said, 'I'm going to control you, Jane. Whatever you do with other men, and I *know* you do, you are going to give your husband everything you have got tonight. Here in this bed, and in my arms. You are going to do as you are told by me.'

Despite myself, I was getting sexually excited too. She was wrong. It was women who turned me on, not men. The only man who interested me was John. And I liked Loveday, even her bottom tasted nice to my lips. She slid down in the bed and said:

'Put your hands in my hair. Like John does. He loves my hair.'

I did as she told me, thinking it was nice and thick and soft and I did not blame John. But he was going to bury his hands in my hair tonight. I kissed Loveday back.

'I'll do what you tell me. But be nice to me, won't you?'

'I'll be nice to you tonight, pet. And I'll let you have the exclusive use of your husband, under my control, but one day I am going to let him have full sexual intercourse with me while you are watching. And you are going to help.'

I did not argue. I kissed her back even more passionately, as if the thought excited me, but I was not going to let that happen.

'So enjoy yourself with John tonight and just lie and think of his strong, thick penis slowly burying itself in me. I'll have your head right down there so you can see. In fact you'll lick me out first to stimulate me for your husband, like I am going to do for you right now.'

Loveday was as good as her word, and when John came in a few minutes later, it was to find me on my back with Loveday's face between my wide open thighs. My hands were deep in Loveday's hair and my eyes closed. He was in bed beside us before I noticed his arrival.

Dear John, we kissed each other passionately and our hands met in Loveday's hair. She was right, John did like her hair. But his other hand was round me and in my hair, grown two inches longer to give him pleasure in its touch. I felt his penis, hard as steel, against my leg, but Loveday was holding it there, her hand around it. And she kept her hand on it all night. Never once was I allowed it unaccompanied by her fingers. Even when it was right inside me, her fingers, Loveday's fingers, were in me too. Either in me or ringing the base of his penis and the open lips of my vagina. And after that first long kiss, she took over my mouth and I had the strange sensation of a male penis ringed by her female fingers, and a woman's kisses instead of John's. In fact she took me over and performed all the duties of the male, except one. It was as if Loveday was making love to me with John's penis.

She kissed him too, long deep kisses to make me jealous, but she would not let him kiss me again.

The other thing she did was to hold his penis back from full penetration every now and then, until I had begged her with my lips and tongue to allow me to have my husband's penis to its full. Again and again, she did it, and it had of course, the effect of prolonging the act.

'Please, please Loveday,' I found myself saying, 'please let him.'

'Well, tell me you love me, Jane.'

'I love you.' I said, as John's penis buried itself to the hilt inside me. But Loveday's fingers were still there. She was almost reading my thoughts with her fingers and her lips, and when John ejaculated inside me it was Loveday who said:

'There child, isn't that nice? You are swimming in wetness aren't you?'

Then she went down and licked me to a climax while John watched. I noticed he was hard again by the time she had finished with my bottom.

We then went to sleep with Loveday lying half across me – so that nothing could happen without her permission, I thought. John was enjoying himself so I was quite happy. It is just as well I was, because Loveday would not have budged an inch to please me. She was pleasing herself, not me.

Chapter 8

Perhaps not surprisingly, we became great friends after that, Loveday and I. I had enjoyed our sex sessions, and I had kept my husband. During the day we were inseparable, we two, and in the evenings we made a threesome. At nights we all slept together – except when one of us had a period – and we had great fun. We were very discreet and although people may have wondered, they did not know.

I never learned to fish, I am afraid, but I watched them fishing and I let them kiss each other as much as they wanted to, as long as I got my share, and I did. From both of them at times. But Loveday would not often let my husband kiss me once we were in bed. She did that for him and monopolized both my mouth and my breasts most of every night. And I enjoyed sex more than I had ever done. As I have already observed, it was not just a man watching me having lesbian sex, which I would not have liked, it was a bi-sexual girl watching and aiding my husband in making love to me. There was a subtle difference. And though she monopolized me during the night, I made it quite plain, in the gentlest possible way, that I drew the line at straight adultery between John and Loveday. We saw she was happy before we went to sleep though, and I let her do anything with John's penis except that one thing. Once, when I was watching my girl friend's throat moving rhythmically as she swallowed everything; with John's penis in her hand and her lips around the end, and me lying quietly beside them, I found myself thinking:

'I could have done with that!' but, instead, I reached over and stroked Loveday's dark hair in an act of friendship. There would be another night.

I had, of course, solved my problem of paying for two homes. Loveday charged me nothing and I had to insist on buying my own drinks. I was told just to sign a chit and forget it. I was, I suppose, in heaven. My lesbian instincts were satisfied to the full and we frequently went to bed with each other in the afternoons. I told John, and he, of course did not mind. Loveday, however, thought she was doing it all behind my husband's back and that gave her a greater sense of pleasure. There was only one thing; she was most firmly the one on top. No way was I allowed to be butch with her. Considering that I am always wanting to make the running, it is amazing how many times I finish up in the receiving position under another woman. One day I will find one, like little Sue, with whom I can fall in love and who will always let me take charge. I liked Sue but I was never in love with her.

Loveday was in love with me, though. She adored me and I could not do anything wrong in her eyes. In turn I got to be very fond of her. We did lots of things besides make love to each other and go fishing. We went to plays and concerts; Loveday even taught me rock climbing in the hills to the south of the hotel. Somehow, I never broke my neck. I was pretty scared at times but my girl friend seemed to enjoy the frightening bits. I once said: 'Look after John if I fall down this bit.' The cliff dropped away a sheer thousand feet beneath me.

I would never do it again, it was only the urgings of Loveday that induced me even to contemplate it. John was surprised. He had never thought me the type. I was not the type, he was quite right about that.

Lisa wrote to me once a week. She seemed to miss me, which was surprising. I thought she would have rather liked being paid for doing very little. The house ought to be like a new pin by now.

Everything comes to an end eventually and, with a week to go before we had to return to the regiment, Loveday said, 'Let me have full sex with John just once, on the last night.'

'All right,' I said. 'As long as I am there. I wouldn't like it if I wasn't.'

'You'll be there all right! Look, this is my plan. I know John wants to, he's always wanted to really. I'll have a word with him and say we will, if you give us permission. Then I'll tell him I will arrange for you to give permission, but he is not to come in while I am persuading you.'

Loveday suddenly laughed. She said my eyes were so wide open with surprise, I looked like one of those little animals at the zoo, that only come out at night and have eyes like saucers.

'What we'll do,' continued Loveday, 'is to go into the other bedroom. I will pretend to smack you with my hand, hard, but I won't actually touch you of course. Then you can start to cry and I will take you back into the other room and you can give permission. Then I will make you stimulate me first. That way it will be much more exciting for John.'

Loveday got my husband on his own by means of arranging a hair appointment for me in the evening, saying they were booked up during the day.

'John,' she asked, alone with him in our room, lying on the bed, 'would you like to make love to me, all the way, if Jane says you can?'

'You know I would,' said my loyal husband.

'Well,' replied Loveday, 'I'll persuade Jane to let you.' She unbuttoned his trouser flies and placed her warm hand on his erect penis. 'But you must not come in whatever you hear.' His penis hardened further. 'I shall be quite tough with her but she'll give you permission.' She employed her favourite trick of trailing her loosened hair over John's penis. 'Do you think you will have the strength of mind to stay out of the room until I have finished with her?'

'Yes,' said John, a tremor to his voice.

Loveday said: 'And do you want me to hit her hard or gently.' She slipped her wet mouth over the end of his penis and sucked. John exploded in her mouth, and as he did so, he said:

'As hard as you like, Loveday!'

The words and the sperm both came out in a rush, and Loveday took everything he gave her. When they had finished, they lay there for a bit, Loveday savouring the pleasure the man's betrayal had given her, because it was a betrayal. John did not know that we had agreed it all between ourselves. But, perhaps, we had tempted him too far. Men are weak about sex.

Came the farewell party at last. And we both saw that John had plenty to drink. We knew the effect it had on him. We were to sleep that night, as we often did, in the wing that was Loveday's private apartments.

Loveday looked at her very best that evening. Her eyes were sparkling with concealed excitement. It was a good thing we had planned this adventure because, otherwise, we would just be feeling rather sad. And it was a good thing we had left it to the end because once they started they would have just gone on. There was no doubt at all about that. Loveday fancied my husband as much as she loved me.

The door of the private apartments closed behind us with a click as the bolt was pushed home.

'Go into the bedroom, John. I have got to have a word with Jane. And don't come out whatever you hear.'

She pushed me into the other bedroom and we quietly undressed. Loveday slipped a nightie over my head but remained in the nude herself. Then she pulled an old fashioned hot water bottle out of a drawer and slapped it with her hand. It sounded just like a hand on bare flesh. She handed me a small bottle of glycerine.

'Your tears,' she whispered.

I am quite a good actress, and I was almost genuinely crying by the sixth slap. Loveday led me into the next room. I looked the part. My hair was falling over my face, wet with tears, and I was sobbing quietly.

'You can make love and go all the way. I give you permission,' I said. John was unashamedly rampant.

'Are you sure you mean that?' said Loveday firmly.

'Yes I mean it,' I replied, miserably. She got on the bed with John and put her arms around him possessively.

'Come here Jane,' demanded Loveday, and I was pulled down on the bed beside them. She grabbed my hair in her hand and pushed my face down to her genitals, which were wet and wide open already.

'Lick me out!' she said. 'And you are going to stay down there for the rest of the night.' She kissed John, who kissed her back, and they lay there for a long while just making love gently to each other. Then came the moment of penetration. I pulled back my husband's foreskin, and then pointed it for him. Slowly, it buried itself in Loveday. They had wanted this for so long, and I was very fond

of Loveday, and I loved John, I did not mind at
all.

Loveday kept her clenched fist, with my hair
twisted round it, in the neighbourhood of John's
bottom the whole time. But apart from that, they
just ignored me until they had finished and they
both climaxed together. Then I was made to dry
them off. The acting was almost professional. I can
remember thinking:

'Loveday and I ought to go on the stage, we are
so good.'

Certainly, John thought his dear wife was serving
under Loveday's orders, and when I told him that I
was not, on the way back home, he looked properly
ashamed.

'And so you should be too!' I declared, laughing.
'Men, they are all the same.'

I missed Loveday, and she missed me even more.
For a while we used to ring each other in the
evenings. We did not meet again but I have often
wondered who she is kissing now. She was so
beautiful she could not just be living a celibate
existence, but perhaps she is. Women, unlike men,
will not settle for just anything.

John, as I thought he would, passed his final
examination. He is generally capable of a spurt at
the end of a course and can catch up with the
others, if he has not been paying attention. And he
had a lot on his mind, my husband, during that
course. But I am not sorry for him. He had a
ball and, at the end, enjoyed something that came

perilously near to the exhibition lesbianism that men adore, and more lesbians eschew.

In the morning, Loveday and I made very gentle and affectionate love to each other and I encouraged John to mount her from behind, taking the weight on his elbows, like a gentleman. I even ran my fingers through her hair to excite him with it and I told her I loved her, and I was so glad to lend her my beloved John, just for once, and she was to enjoy it without thinking I would be jealous. To tell the truth, I was not jealous, not the slightest bit. I had kept my man. I had a beautiful woman making love to me as if I were the most precious thing the world had ever known, and John was enjoying a woman he had hankered after and had so far resisted. I felt he deserved it, if only for his fidelity to date. I encouraged him to do it properly and make love to her verbally, without regard to my presence.

'Tell Loveday she is pretty John,' I said. 'Make her realize that you do love her, and it's not just lust.'

And John did just that. He was very sweet with her, and so was I. I was actually feeling rather sorry for her because I had still got John and there was also little Lisa back home (who had written such dutiful and affectionate letters while I was away that I had a feeling I could manage her too). Whereas poor Loveday was losing us both, and I knew she loved me dearly. The only stumbling block was John. She would want John every night if she came to live with us and I drew a line at that. Once, yes, but every night, no. Poor Loveday,

I cuddled her harder as she responded to John's vigorous thrusts. We two climaxed together and John sometime later. As we had our orgasms simultaneously, I think we had almost forgotten my husband, we were concentrating on each other.

John had to report to his temporary unit before departure while Loveday and I lay together in bed, and thanked each other for what we had received. It felt a bit like grace after a feast, and it certainly had been a feast. I enjoyed my sex with Loveday, and loved having sex with John while she watched – if watched is the right word. Her fingers were everywhere.

As we drove up the road towards home, we both felt sad. I know Loveday did too, because she told me so on the phone that night. But there was another reason why it could not go on for ever, although I was very fond of her and I knew she genuinely loved me. I wanted to be the one on top, a female yes, but on top. One day I would achieve it and then I knew I would be happy.

9

Chapter 9

Little Lisa was so pleased to see us on our return. She said she had been lonely by herself and that she was glad that we were back. As I kissed her on the cheek I smelt that soft, fresh baby smell I had noticed when I said goodbye to her. So much of physical attraction between human beings is based on the report of the olfactory nerve, and Lisa smelled so sweet.

The quarters were spotlessly clean. She was a good girl and had worked just as well without supervision as if I had been there. Mark you, I am never one to overbear my staff. I would rather not have a girl if I had to watch her all the time.

Lisa had lost a little weight I thought; it was puppy fat anyway, and her fair hair was long and shiny. She looked very German, especially if she put her hair in plaits. I liked it loose and told her so. I soon unplaited it for her and brushed it out. She was pleased I took notice of her I think, because she bought me a little present that very afternoon. It was just a nylon scarf, but it was a pretty one and it was sweet of her. I took her in my arms and kissed her, properly this time, and she kissed me back. Here we go again, I thought, as I ran my fingers through her hair.

'Always have it loose, Lisa, so I can do that.' I said. 'Do you know you smell nice?'

Lisa flushed. 'I'm glad,' she said. 'And I'm glad you're back. I missed you.'

I formed the impression that Lisa had been jealous. She knew just a little about the purpose of my visit and wondered why I had stayed away so long. Feminine intuition worked out the rest, I think. As for me, I was secretly dying to get back to my old stance, having a girl friend who was sexually subordinate to me rather than the other way round, as it had been with Loveday.

The very next afternoon Lisa had trouble with her bra. One of the straps had broken, and I suggested she undid her dress while I mended it. After a moment or two I said:

'I can't do it unless you take it off.' And, without waiting for an answer, undid the clips at the back and removed it. Her breasts, as I thought they might be, were beautiful. They were pink tipped and perfectly shaped. They were heavy but did not droop or sag at all. She was very young, of course. I cupped them in my hands and kissed her as she turned her face towards me.

'Lisa, come to bed,' I said.

'I've got to iron the spare bedroom sheets, haven't I?' she replied.

'Yes, but they can wait. I can't.'

There was no further argument. She wanted to

come to bed. We undressed and made love all afternoon, me on top. She was very pretty, very willing, and this was her first bi-sexual experience. I was happy because I was back where I wanted to be and Loveday and her passion for me receded into the past.

I came to the conclusion the only reason that I had never made love to Lisa before was that I was frightened she would not work well if I did. What she had done, entirely on her own, whilst I had been away, convinced me that my fears were groundless. And so they proved to be. For over a year we were lovers from time to time, and she never let me down.

The thing I liked most of all about her was the beautiful scent of her body. Even if she had been working hard on a hot day she still smelt nice.

Lisa was my only German girlfriend, except for finishing school, which seemed a long time ago now. Our love life was quite uncomplicated and matter-of-fact. Perhaps it was not as exciting as the one I had enjoyed with Loveday, but more to my inclination.

John was glad. He says he likes me to be happy, and I think he does.

From Lisa I learned a lot about her country. Up till then I had had little to do with the teeming millions of north Germany. The British army, though living in great amity with the local population, conducted their own social lives largely apart from them.

I met Lisa's family, who had originated in Latvia, and were descended from the original

Teuton knights who once conquered and then governed the three Baltic states, rather as the English did in Ireland. She was the youngest of four children, all boys except for her, and her overweening interests were pop music and writing to pen pals. She wrote to one in Canada in French, two in Australia in English and one in Japan in German, he replying in the same language. Lisa did not seem to have been very activated by boys as such and said she found my caresses quite enough for her at this stage of her life. I certainly would not have stood in her way had there been a boy she wanted.

I was lying in bed with her one morning when John, who had left for duty at 6 a.m., came home and announced that he was off for a week with his unit. He hesitated and I knew what he wanted. I was just about to slide out of bed and go to our room, when emboldened by the Loveday experiment, he moved towards the girl's bed in which we lay.

'I don't mind,' said Lisa, who had been told that my husband knew about our lesbian relationship, and before long John was making love to me in his usual fashion. I was quite ready for him, of course, thanks to the activities of my girlfriend and so also, my fingers told me, was Lisa. I noticed he was stroking the girl's long blonde hair with his left hand with his right hand in mine. Quickly I brought Lisa's mouth over to mine and with my right hand occupied and guarded her vagina which, in the circumstances, ought to be regarded as sacrosanct, I thought.

John buried his face in her soft, sweet-smelling hair, which gave him a further dimension to his passion. The girl and I just kissed. That was as far as I let it go, but Lisa seemed to be rather pleased to be trusted by me, to be in bed with my husband. Seeing she was so young and pretty it was a bit of a risk and I quietly decided not to take that risk too often. Not even with faithful John.

I had a climax and, quite frankly, it was with the girl and not with my husband. It was a vast improvement on mere imagination, for I had often made love to Lisa in John's arms, in my thoughts, and when John had gone, I told her so.

'When I am married,' she said, 'I shall sometimes do the same. I often find myself attracted to girls and women and, perhaps, that is the best way to satisfy the urge where it exists.'

I think, in many ways, she was quite right. Not all husbands are as accommodating as mine. But I enjoyed that particular little episode. The only trouble was that we both went to sleep in each other's arms and not a stroke of work was done until after noon, when we made some smoked salmon sandwiches and opened a bottle of wine. Then, as Lisa had to go to see her mother, I had to tidy up, but it was well worth it and I made no secret of the fact.

'I'll work twice as hard tomorrow. Don't worry,' she said, as she kissed me affectionately and then gave me that bright, instant smile, I shall always remember her for. If I think German girls are nice, and I do, little Lisa has a lot to do with my attitude. As far as I am concerned, she and I concluded an

Anglo-German entente. I missed her terribly when we had to part and I think she missed me. For a long time we wrote to each other – nice, long, loving letters full of the little stories of everyday events with which we had regaled each other in between the household chores. Her family had to move to another part of Germany and Lisa was considered too young to stay behind alone. I gave her a puppy as a goodbye present and she wept in its fur. Like most Germans, she loved animals and I am quite sure that small dog had a good home for the rest of its life.

I have often wondered, did the girl's mother detect the secret fascination that existed between her young daughter and me? Only John had seen my fingers, the fingers of my left hand enhanced with a gold wedding ring, entwined in the girl's golden hair, but women have a sixth sense about these matters. I only know that Lisa did not want to leave, but family ties are strong in that part of continental Europe.

Looking back on it all, I may not have been in love with Lisa, but I did love her and, possibly, by some inadvertent word or gesture I betrayed this.

❖ 10 ❖

Chapter 10

One of the most successful British contractors in the town in which we lived had a wife, Geraldine, who was the most amusing woman I have ever met. Her conversation was frequently outrageous, but it was always funny. She was, naturally, very popular with most people and I was rather flattered when I noticed she was taking an interest in me. She was about 30, with light brown, curly hair and a way of moving which reminded me of one of those civet cats you see at the zoo. When she smiled the smile went right to her eyes. I found myself being attracted to her and I wondered if she was femme. I had a feeling there was a lesbian streak to her nature, but I was far from sure. Apart from being happily married, or so I assumed, she did not seem to react to men to any great extent. Given a chance, I would try, I remember thinking.

The chance came when she invited me to go to the opera with her. Verdi's 'Aida' was my favourite, so I accepted at once. Almost as soon as we took our seats she put her hand on my lap to hold my hand. My heart missed a beat, and we held hands during the whole of the production.

As soon as it was over I said to her: 'Come home to supper with me. My husband will be in bed by now, and we can have a quiet talk together.'

As soon as I had closed the front door behind us I thought I would make the first move. We were still holding hands which, to say the least, is not at all usual with grown women, if they are both heterosexual.

I took hold of her other hand as well, intending to embrace her. I had just said, 'Thanks for a lovely evening,' when she kissed me.

It was a shy, almost childish kiss, which I returned quietly for a full ten seconds, then I slipped my tongue in her mouth. From her response, I knew I had won. I do not know how long we kissed but after a while I realized she was limp in my arms in passive consent. If I had not pushed her against the wall she would have slipped to the floor. But I had a better place in mind than the floor. Bed was where she was going. I moved my pelvis suggestively against hers, and she opened her mouth just a little more. I could almost feel her warmth through her dress. Geraldine was more than ready for anything I was planning, I concluded.

I wondered if her husband knew what his wife was like. He would not find out from me, anyway, but I was resolved that Geraldine was going to be unfaithful to him tonight – if making love to another woman is being unfaithful. Personally, I have never thought so, but some people do. I had a feeling her husband would. He was a reserved and rather formal businessman who had been a naval officer.

Then I noticed Geraldine's kiss was scented, she had prepared for this moment, I mused. I wondered how much experience she had had. Was I the first woman who had ever kissed her like this? I hoped so, but I wanted her badly, even if I was not the first.

We never got to having that supper. I led her into the guest room by her hand, and switched off the light.

I turned off the light, I concluded later, because I thought she would be shy. Nothing could be further from the truth. Once we were in bed, naked in each other's arms, she was affection itself. But I was careful to begin with, in case Geraldine thought that lesbianism was all just a sisterhood of platonic kisses. I felt I must not alarm her by being too bold too fast.

It was some time before I even dared to take one of her nipples in my mouth. To my gratification, she encouraged me by stroking my hair with her hand and, in due course, I allowed my fingers to touch her pubic hair and then her vagina which, to my faint surprise, was wide open and ready for me. I petted Geraldine with gentle care, as she returned my kisses with growing ardour. Then suddenly she pushed me over on my back and went down on me.

With the practised ease of the professional, she slipped her tongue into me, opening my legs wide. I had my hands in her hair, running my fingers through her soft curls, when my arms seemed to become heavy and I let go. A second later I climaxed under Geraldine's probing and, quite obviously, experienced tongue.

And so it went on through the night. She made all the running. The huntress had become the hunted. Geraldine did not even want to go home. She had told her husband she was going to spend the night with friends. She had obviously planned my seduction from the start to finish.

She even admitted it later. 'I thought you were butch, so I pretended to be femme to get you because I wanted you so much. But you enjoyed it, didn't you?'

I had to admit that I did. After that we never actually made love again, at least not all the way. We were both butch and became great friends, finding girlfriends for each other.

For a long time we hunted as a pair and, as we had similar tastes and inclinations, we got on fine.

Geraldine even admitted to fantasizing about girls while her husband made love to her, just as I did.

Bit by bit, I found out the story of her life. Geraldine had left college to join the Prison Service, and served for a while as a Probationary Prison Officer. She showed me a picture of herself, aged 20, in her uniform. Forbidding though the uniform was, she looked most attractive in it, and some of the female prisoners in the women's open gaol thought so too.

The moment she arrived on the floor of the prison she felt the longing in the eyes of one or two of the older lags. Several of them, she noticed, had little harems of adoring female followers.

In the world of women in a prison, lesbianism, open or latent, flourishes. It is, of course, officially forbidden and sternly discouraged but love laughs at locksmiths. It went on just the same.

There was a queen bee who Geraldine noticed eyeing her. Her name was Millie, at least that is what the other women called her, and she had three girlfriends in her supporting team of followers.

Millie was a big woman, handsome in her way, with short hair and a full figure. Her age was given as 40 in the prison records, and her crime was living on the immoral earnings of other women.

One night when Geraldine was on duty, her supervisor, a senior prison officer, asked if she would cover for her while she slipped out to see her man friend. She gave Geraldine a telephone number to ring if anyone important asked for her, and said she would be back by 6 a.m.

Apart from being mildly surprised that anyone so unattractive as Prison Officer Martin could have a boyfriend, Geraldine's only feeling was pleasure at being trusted to take charge on her own, after only a few weeks' experience.

Sitting in the office writing up the Night Report, she was startled by a white-faced girl, one of Millie's little acolytes, arriving to say: 'Millie's ill. Will you please come and see her?'

Now, Millie was in the one cell kept for emergencies. Her offence had been to strike an officer. Actually, she had only flapped the head cook with a drying-up cloth in an argument about the menu, and was going to be let out the next day with a caution.

The screws, Geraldine noticed, were very careful with Millie. She was a law unto herself.

She hurried along behind the girl until they got to the cell door which she unlocked, opened, and then shut and locked behind her.

Millie was lying on the bed groaning convincingly.

'Poor Millie,' said Geraldine. 'What is wrong? Can I help?'

'I think I've got appendicitis,' was the reply.

'Let me have a look,' said Geraldine, leaning over the woman as she unbuttoned her pyjama jacket. She remembered noticing how beautifully shaped Millie's full, heavy breasts were as she placed her hand on her stomach.

'No, further down,' Millie said, looking Geraldine full in the face.

Millie pulled her pyjama trousers right down, to reveal a bush of black, curly pubic hair which Geraldine saw was damp. At the same time she took the girl's arm in her hand and placed her fingers in her vagina.

'That's where it is,' she said, wantonly.

Geraldine panicked, but her wrist was held in a grip of iron. The woman's vagina was as deep as the Cheddar Gorge, she remembered thinking, as Millie's other arm enveloped her and brought her forcibly down on to the bed.

'No, Millie, stop it, this is quite immoral,' was all she could think of saying before her lips were pressed to Millie's and a tongue was inserted into her mouth, effectively preventing further protest.

Outside the cell a small knot of women were

standing silently listening. One was watching through the observation hole in the door.

In a few minutes Millie had the girl's uniform off and her underclothes strewn across the floor. She was immensely strong and very experienced. Geraldine was like a child in her capable hands.

Before long the women outside the door could see their young officer spreadeagled naked on the bed with the older woman on top of her. Millie's torso undulated on Geraldine's and their mouths were glued together.

'She hadn't a chance,' one of the women whispered with barely suppressed amusement, as Geraldine's muffled orgasm could even be heard through the thickness of the oak door.

Millie kept her there on the bed with her until 5 a.m., a good seven hours later, saying: 'The old screw won't be back until 6 a.m. I know her. She's man mad.'

Geraldine was licked out, served with a smuggled dildo that Millie had procured, and Millie sat on her face until she had an orgasm as well.

Then she was allowed to dress and return to duty without, she thought, anyone knowing. But it was all round the prison by breakfast time. Millie had seduced a young screw. And within three weeks of her joining the Prison Service. Clever old Millie! The women cheered her wherever she went and Millie openly boasted of her prowess.

'She was a pushover. I didn't even have to court her.'

Geraldine was silly, but we are often silly when

we are young. She liked it so much she went back
for more, three nights later.

Then every third night, when Prison Officer
Martin was on her clandestine assignations, Geraldine would let herself into Millie's cell. They had
let her out, once, but the visiting magistrates had
put her back in again for 28 days. This was fine for
Geraldine.

She suddenly realized why she had been subcon-
sciously impelled to join the Women's Prison
Service, she was a lesbian. From the authority's
point of view, that was probably the worst of all
reasons for choosing that particular vocation or
career.

The first time she let herself in to the cell again,
Millie just looked up from her bed and said:

'You have come back for some more have you?'

'I've come to cheer you up, Millie.'

'Well take off that ugly uniform child, and your
panties, and get into bed. I thought you would
come back for some more. You liked it didn't you?'

Geraldine did as she was told and surrendered
herself completely to Millie's lust for a younger
woman. And the small group of women prisoners
took turns to watch through the peep hole, obviously enjoying the spectacle.

Geraldine said afterwards that it never occurred
to her that they would do that.

'I would have died of shame if I had known they
were all watching. The things Millie did to me. She
knew of course, I realize now. That is why my legs
were held open, right under the light, so they could
see everything. She had put them up to it. Someone

even took a photograph of me being licked out by Millie. She kept it in her wallet and showed it to everyone in the prison.'

It could not last. After seven or eight nocturnal visits to get laid by Millie, the Governor got to hear about it. She was the last to hear, but when she did, she acted swiftly. Geraldine's probationary period of service came to an abrupt end.

Even then her sense of humour did not desert her.

'The Governor said I was unsuitable because I had taken advantage of the weakness of women in an unnatural situation. Weakness! I was the one who was weak. She was as tough as an old boot. And they tell me she just laughed when she heard I'd got chucked out because of her. Oh well, at least I enjoyed it while it lasted. If only people would keep their traps shut.'

Geraldine managed to get out of the Prison Service without any adverse report against her. The Governor knew all right, but she could not prove it and Millie denied everything when challenged to her face in the Governor's office. Then she boasted about it again as soon as she got outside, in the hearing of one of the screws, who was a lesbian too, and could not care less as long as she was clear. She specialized in girls on remand for minor offences like shoplifting, too frightened to say no to a prison officer.

Geraldine let the dust settle for a while and then, having got some good references from the local vicar and others, applied to join the W.R.N.S.

To her delight she was accepted and, in due course, rose to the rating of Petty Officer. She found that there were one or two lesbians in the Service. They were all very discreet. It was death to be found out. The Navy did not approve of that sort of thing.

The best way, Geraldine found, was to go baby-sitting for a married officer, with another girl as a companion.

'We used to hop into bed as soon as they had got out of the door. And by not being on Service premises, there was little or no risk.'

Came the day Geraldine was drafted to the Far East for two years. She quickly managed to fix it that Molly, a little Wren rating who was her current friend, got drafted too, and they sailed in a troop transport from Southampton.

As they sailed down the Solent, Geraldine had her first chance to look over her fellow passengers. The one that attracted her most was a Third Officer W.R.N.S., who was nominally in charge of the Wren draft, and Geraldine's immediate superior.

She was very young, a cypher officer, straight from school. Cypher Queens, as they were called by the Wrens, did not have to go through the ranks but were commissioned from shore on their educational qualifications alone.

Caroline was her Christian name, Geraldine discovered from the Admiralty list, and she was as fresh as a drop of morning dew: a petite little figure, blue grey eyes and soft fair hair, worn straight and tucked under – sensuously, Geraldine thought.

'If I pulled it down, it would fall below her collar,

and that's against Navy regulations. I bet that's the first thing Ma'am says on arrival!'

Geraldine was second-in-command of the draft and so she saw a lot of Caroline and was glad to find they got on well.

She did not rate her chances very high but she was resolved to make a pass at the Third Officer. 'I can always play it pear-shaped so I can withdraw under a smoke screen if it isn't going to work! Nothing ventured, nothing gained,' Geraldine thought. 'I'd give my eye teeth to have her in bed for just one night.'

The sea was calm and even the dreaded Bay of Biscay failed to produce its usual storm. Geraldine contented herself with having Molly in her cabin most nights. Even this was quite contrary to regulations, but no one found out. Molly, who was 18 and had just joined, was a soft touch for her Wren Petty Officer girlfriend who, by now, was an experienced and skilful lesbian.

As she got older, Geraldine found herself orientating from femme to butch. She had been very much femme as a girl in the arms of Millie but, like a lot of women with similar inclinations, she changed with seniority to wanting to make the running, and be the one on top, as she put it. And she was certainly on top with Molly, who was not much more than a schoolgirl, but very highly sexed and willing to do anything she was asked to do. Especially as being in the good books of the Petty Officer in charge of the regulation of the naval draft meant you got an easy passage.

Molly had brown eyes, dark brown hair in a bob

and fringe, and came from Ulster. Geraldine had broken her in within a week of joining the Wrens, and taught her all she knew on the first night. After that they never looked back.

Lying in the bunk together, Geraldine told Molly about her thoughts and plans for Caroline.

'But she's an officer. You can't do that.'

'Well, I am going to have a go and if I make it I am going to involve you too.'

'Me?'

'Yes, you, darling,' Geraldine replied. She's going to be Quarters' Officer when we get there and I am going to get her to ask for me as her Petty Officer, and you as her Wren steward. Then we'll keep it all in the family and no one will ever be any wiser as to what's going on. Leave it to me.'

Geraldine went down on her Wren girlfriend and brought her off. Molly liked her sex and was quite uncomplicated about it. She would do what Geraldine told her when the time came. And she did not find the thought of having sex with Caroline other than pleasant. She supposed her Wren Petty Officer knew what she was talking about.

Geraldine noticed during the next few days that, although the ship was packed with good-looking Army officers, Caroline came up from the mess as soon as meals were finished and read a book in her cabin or dealt with the official papers, which seemed to materialize even here, out on the ocean. Geraldine took every opportunity to help her young officer, and the cabin virtually became an office.

Geraldine put the idea of her being second-in-command to Caroline when they got to their destination, as well as just the naval draft.

'You'll need someone like me to keep you out of trouble,' she said, 'Quarters' Officer is a difficult job, especially if you have got to keep your watches on cypher traffic as well. I'll see you are all right. I am nearly old enough to be your mother.'

Geraldine smiled. She was not, of course, but it sounded good.

Caroline seemed pleased at the offer of motherhood. She looked very beautiful in her white naval uniform, with sunlight from the porthole illuminating her golden hair. Geraldine touched her on the cheek with her fingers, which was fairly bold of her. But Caroline had not been in the Navy long enough to be inhibited by her rank. She just said: 'Thank you Geraldine, that would be fine.'

Caroline had started to call Geraldine by her Christian name when they were alone, she noticed. It was a good sign.

The breakthrough came a few days later. Geraldine was helping Caroine to close a porthole, on a sudden increase in wind strength. Standing behind her, screwing up her clip, she found the girl in her arms, limp and willing. Geraldine buried her face in Caroline's fair hair and said, almost involuntarily:

'I love you.'

She pushed her down on the bunk and unbuttoned her uniform jacket. Geraldine was already in her shirt sleeves as she got in beside her young officer. The door was locked. Geraldine always locked the door. Without hesitation they kissed.

Unknown to each other they had both been longing for this, regulations or no regulations.

After a while they both undressed and explored each other's bodies. Geraldine was very much in charge though. It was she who eventually licked Caroline out, not the other way round. She said, as she did so:

'You really are a blonde, Ma'am, you are even blonde down here.'

They both laughed, and Caroline said:

'Don't call me Ma'am in bed, it sounds silly.'

'No, of course I won't, darling, but I promise you one thing, when we are on duty, never by the slightest familiarity will the world ever know what we have done together. I shall be the most respectful subordinate in the Service.'

Five minutes after that remark, Caroline gave way to a tumultuous climax induced by Geraldine's experienced tongue.

This was Caroline's very first affair with a woman, she admitted later, and it was super so far. She had had a boyfriend for a brief period, but he had just succeeded in hurting her physically and mentally, and she was ripe for seduction by a lesbian. That the lesbian should be her own Petty Officer complicated matters, but they would find a way to make love without anyone knowing. After all, male officers did not hesitate to take advantage of Wren ratings if they can get away with it, she reasoned. So she returned Geraldine's embraces with interest, compound interest at that.

'Are there many lesbians in the Wrens?' Caroline asked one afternoon.

'You will always get some whenever you get a lot of women together, but there are not very many in our Service,' replied Geraldine.

'There are a few enthusiastic AC/DC ones of course,' she added with a laugh, 'that's why I should like to introduce you to Molly, she's one of us, and if she were to be your Wren steward, she would act as a safety barrier between us and the rest of the Service. Otherwise, our relationship may become known through an unsympathetic Wren. With Molly we have nothing to fear.'

Geraldine was enjoying her voyage. Work in the morning, sex with Caroline most afternoons, usually a party or a film in the evening, and sex with Molly most nights. This trip could go on for ever as far as she was concerned, especially as she had Caroline well under her thumb by now. Caroline enjoyed being sexually dominated by an older woman, as much as Geraldine liked dominating her.

And outside the cabin it was all 'Yes Ma'am, no Ma'am,' standing to attention and saluting. It was the contrast that made it fun and appealed to Geraldine's sense of humour. Caroline did not seem to worry about the dangers which, as Molly said, did not exist if they were all sensible and played ball.

'I will, anyway,' said Molly, and this was faithfully reported to Caroline.

'I am going to bring Molly up here this afternoon,' announced Geraldine firmly, one morning. Caroline turned pink, and she looked radiant in her Third Officer's well-cut uniform. Geraldine noticed she was breathing faster than usual, but she made no reply.

Promptly at 2 p.m. with everyone not on watch enjoying what the Navy called a Make and Mend, Geraldine let Molly into the cabin and locked the door behind her.

Molly was looking particularly pretty, Geraldine thought; with her brown hair freshly washed and wearing just the right amount of scent and make-up.

'This is your Wren steward to be,' said Geraldine 'she would like to be called Molly, if you agree.'

'How nice of you to volunteer,' replied Caroline, rather formally. Geraldine could almost hear the girl's heart beating.

'Sit down in the chair, and Molly will do your hair. She is a trained hairdresser amongst other things.'

Molly had been carefully briefed by Geraldine during a sex session the night before, and she proceeded to unpin her officer's fair hair and brush it through. Geraldine sat and watched.

Gradually, it became apparent that Molly was not brushing her hair, but fondling it. Her hands slowly moved from Caroline's hair to her neck and then, unbuttoning the front of her shirt, to her breasts, which she removed from their supporting bra, before cupping them in her hands.

Geraldine said, 'Now Molly,' and Caroline looked up, to be kissed on the mouth. Geraldine undressed them both, and then herself and, getting into the bunk with her back against the bulkhead, took them both in her arms. Molly was on top.

Quietly, for the next half hour she supervised their love making, in the end pushing Molly down between Caroline's thighs. Geraldine propped herself up on her elbow to watch her young officer's enraptured face. After she had climaxed in Molly's mouth, Geraldine said:

'You know, I think a woman looks her most beautiful at the second of orgasm. You certainly do.'

Caroline was too exhausted to reply, and all three of them lay there and slept until tea-time, just as they were.

It had taken a fair amount of organizing, thought Geraldine, with dates and everything, but it had been worth it. Now she had broken the ice it would be much easier. She then made love to both of them, one after the other, Caroline first.

Just before Molly left, she said to her Third Officer:

'You needn't worry, I'll never tell anyone. And I'll be a good and respectful Wren outside this room!' She went up to Caroline and boldly kissed her on the mouth.

Geraldine thought the picture of two young women, much the same age, both in neat uniforms, one blonde and one brunette, kissing each other without shame, was quite beautiful. She wished she had been allowed to photograph them, a thought she put behind her as soon as it arrived on the screen of her mind.

Instead, she went up and kissed Caroline too, deeply and possessively.

'It will be all right now,' she said. 'We have an

unbeatable system as long as we love each other. So here's to us.'

When they all arrived at their destination, Caroline was whisked off first, and it was some time before Geraldine saw her again. She was, however, sent for by the Chief Wren, and told she was in charge of the Wren Quarters, and a day later Molly was given her billet of Wren servant and steward to the Third Officer, Wren Quarters. It had all fallen into place, to Geraldine's delight.

Geraldine told me that she often used to make love to Molly with Caroline watching, and vice versa, but that was as public as she wanted to go. She said that she would never let a man watch. 'I have often wondered why? Why make this differentiation? And I have never come to any firm conclusion. I only know that to make love to a girl with a woman with whom one is in sympathy, a lesbian too, watching or even lying close alongside her, lips to the girl's cheek, adds zest to the act.

'There were times when I would lick Molly out and encourage Caroline to kiss her while I did it. When you have a female threesome the permutations, if not endless, are numerous indeed.

'We had a lovely time during that commission – that's what the Wrens call a period of duty in a ship or shore station – and no one ever knew or guessed what we did. Some people prefer to come out of the closet, as they say, but I prefer to stay where I am, in feigned respectability, with my lurid past and unconventional present known only to the cognescenti.'

Geraldine even said she had a soft spot for Millie.

'She was a rough old sort and, had I met her outside, she'd have had me on the streets, between bouts of lesbianism, but she took immense trouble to bring me to orgasm in her arms. She was impossible, and she planned the whole business of my seduction, but I couldn't help liking her, despite everything. After all she didn't do me any harm. I had a much better time in the W.R.N.S. than I'd ever have had in the Prison Service.'

And they never did get found out. They spent two years on the station, and then Caroline and Molly returned to the United Kingdom at the end of their engagements. They were still living together in a cottage deep in the English countryside when Geraldine, left in the East, met a naval officer who was going to leave to take up a business career and, to everyone's surprise, married him.

This takes Geraldine to the point where she met me. We had a brief affair, and then a long, amusing friendship. I shall always feel kindly about Geraldine and remember her stories, and her involved lesbian plots. To think, when we first met, I thought she was a little innocent. The invisibility of homosexuality never ceases to surprise me. I think the invisible way is better and certainly more exciting than being brazen about it.

I have said elsewhere that I do not much like women, although I need them. But I do like lesbian women. We are a sort of sisterhood and very loyal to each other, when we are not stealing each other's partners.

After all, the moment of domination in lesbian sex is giving supreme pleasure to another women.

With a man it is when he has pleasure. I am speaking of course, in general. There are exceptions to every rule, but I love the feeling of comradeship, superficial or otherwise, that follows a lesbian orgy, a successful threesome carried through to its logical conclusion. And lesbian love, for those lucky enough to achieve it, is the most beautiful thing in the world.

People may frown at lesbianism, but it is one of the expressions of liberty that has made the western world what it is. In the modern era it all started on the island of Lesbos and it is Greek civilization which is the foundation of all we know today.

Geraldine was a great philosopher and we spent many hours discussing the world in which we lived. I may not like the generality of my own sex all the time, as I suppose I should, but I liked her very much and I shall remember her humour and wisdom as long as I live. Dear Geraldine, she was one of the most universally popular women I have ever met. Men liked her and her girlfriends worshipped the ground she walked on.

She was, of course, a feminist but she was not an aggressive one. Geraldine believed in equal opportunities for women, to use the well-worn phrase, but she did not believe in mothers abandoning their children to professional minders if they got in the way of a career. She would have made a wonderful mother if she had been able to have the child she and her husband wanted.

'Men can be very gentle with children, some men that is, but most children notice that women have softer hands, softer skins, softer hair, softer eyes, and bosoms to weep on. So, when they are little, they prefer their mothers, though I know,' she said, 'it is "Mum, mum," when they are miserable, and "Dad, dad," when they are happy.'

Geraldine admitted that women were often five or six years behind men in their professional careers if they raised a family but, she said, women had their own reward. Men tattoo the word 'Mum' on their arms and men and women die with the word 'Mother' on their lips. 'Some women think that is not enough, but I think it is,' she said. 'Love is beyond price, whether it is the love of a child, a man or another woman.'

Her favourite story from the history of the Jewish people was that of Ruth and Naomi. If only one knew the whole truth, she would say, you would find that Ruth had a lesbian relationship with her mother-in-law, either physical or mental, or both.

'Where you go, I will go, and where you stay, I will stay . . . nothing but death shall divide us' – it is the beautiful story of the love of two women, which will fascinate people as long as the world rolls round.

'Perhaps it was only mental,' Geraldine said. 'Who knows? But it was love.'

Her defence of her deeds, which needed no defence as far as I was concerned, were contained in the words of the poet Thomas Campion and which she often quoted:

'My sweetest Lesbia, let us live and love,
And although the sager sort our deeds reprove,
Let us not weigh them. . . .'

❧11❧

Chapter 11

There was an organization in the local area run by a charitable trust, which advertised adventure training weeks for boys and girls from the United Kingdom. The girls' wing was not far from where we lived.

Every summer we had batches of schoolgirls for a week's training in adventure and sport in the spacious German countryside. The whole system was run on army lines, although it was nothing to do with the army. The youngsters were given a uniform of sorts, which saved their own clothes from damage, and they looked quite smart as they set out every morning on their projects and schedules. It was all well organized and everyone seemed to enjoy themselves. They were all called Adventure Cadets and the wardens were Sergeants and Sergeant Majors. It was a sort of gimmick.

I was friendly with the senior warden who looked after the girl cadets. I knew her as Eve. She and I recognized each other for what we were from the start, although we were very circumspect and not a word passed between us on the subject. Eve had been in the army as a career soldier and had come out at 40 with a pension. She was one of the sort the Services seem to have quite a lot of, good-looking enough to make you wonder why they never married. I knew why this one had never married, but it was not the desire to secure an army pension that motivated her.

But Eve had been very careful. There was never a suspicion of scandal in her life. Her girlfriends were all German and her love life was conducted well away from the army.

Then one week, a young girl, with one sweep of her eye lashes changed all that. A most beautiful girl cadet arrived, for some reason, for two consecutive weeks' adventure training, and was to spend the weekend under the charge of the Sergeant-Major. Her name was Karen.

'I can think of safer places, Eve.' I said, with a friendly smile. Eve and I could tease each other, but this was the first time I had ventured out on this particular limb.

'Yes, so can I when she's as pretty as that. I could eat her. But the trouble is the age gap is too great. I am 42 and the girl is 17. But if you helped me we might make it. You are a lot younger than I am.'

'Help you? How?' I asked with feigned innocence. She opened the door of her office and invited me in.

'If you turn up late at night, saying your car has broken down, I'll save the day by offering to put you up for the night. Then I will set the girl a bad example by carrying on with you. Then, later, you can take her to bed. There's a double bed in the guest room,' volunteered Eve, with crisp army efficiency. 'She will have had a good few gins poured down her by then.'

'Yes, and at *la moment critique*, you slide into bed and take over.' I replied.

'Correct,' said Eve, 'and, moreover, if you leave the light on there is a two-way mirror from the next bedroom so I can watch the whole thing, and know when to intervene. I'll let you enjoy yourself with her first though. I'd love to watch Karen in your arms.'

'Well, I'm game. She's the most beautiful girl the Adventure Cadets have ever produced. But what happens if she tells her mother all about it when she returns?' I asked. 'You don't want to get the sack do you? You are sitting pretty here with a well-paid job, a company car, a company house and a pension.'

'There isn't a mother. She was brought up by an older sister. But she won't tell. They never do, if they've enjoyed it. And she'll enjoy it.'

I could see the attractions of this girl were outweighing Eve's normally cautious attitude to her personal inclinations and her fear of the problems it might cause her. As a lesbian myself, I sympathized with her because I could see both the attraction and the dangers. To hell with the dangers – nothing ventured, nothing gained, I thought. The girl's beauty had hooked me, too.

At that moment Karen knocked at the office door.

'Come in Karen,' said Eve, in a more kindly tone of voice than she normally used. I could detect the difference, although she was always fairly pleasant to the girl cadets, who quite obviously liked her in return.

Karen marched in and saluted, every inch the soldier girl on duty. She was breathtakingly lovely. She had a flawless complexion, her eyes were violet-tinged, and her mouth a Cupid's bow. She was slim but with well-formed breasts which showed up even under a military tunic; her hair was straight and thick, a rich English mouse, held well up from her collar by dent of many pins. It nearly fell down when she saluted, I noticed with rather unkind amusement. Eve, I knew from well developed feminine intuition, was mentally undressing the girl. Eve would not take long to get the girl's hair down given the chance, I mused, pins or no pins.

'S'art Major,' said Karen dutifully.

'You will report to my quarters when the rest of your unit returns to the U.K. this evening. I have been ordered to take care of you until Monday morning, when you join the new formation of Adventure Cadets.'

'S'art Major,' said Karen, like a little toy soldier in a musical comedy. She saluted and turned smartly about.

When she had left the office Eve said: 'I could tear off her uniform.'

'You probably will,' I replied, but I had to confess that I felt that way too, and promised faithfully to have a contrived mechanical breakdown outside Eve's house at 10 p.m. that evening. We were to be conspirators in the night and our mutual aim was the seduction of innocence. It was planned like an army exercise and I felt it really ought to be detailed in Part II Orders, like any other exercise:

'O.R.s will fall in at 2200 hours. Dress, pyjamas. Toothbrushes will be provided.'

Then Eve pulled me into the next room, which had no outside window. It was more like a large cupboard than a room, although it had a light from a single bulb. There she kissed me full on the mouth, feeling my breasts boldly as she did so.

'Promise me you'll get her for me if you can,' she said.

'I will, don't worry. I don't usually fail, and frankly, I want her myself as much as you do,' I replied helpfully.

Eve swung round and turned the key in the lock. I noticed the key was already on the inside of the door.

'Let me look,' she said. It was more of an order than a request. I unbuttoned my dress, letting it fall to my waist, and removed my bra, baring my full, heavy breasts to her gaze.

'This is what I am going to do tonight,' said Eve. She turned me round and cupped my naked breasts in her hands. 'And let Karen see me do it.' Then she put one hand down my front until she found my pubic hair, which she suggestively combed with her fingers. I turned my head round and offered her my mouth to be kissed again. Eve was so masterly in her handling I really did, on this occasion, feel overwhelmingly feminine. I can sometimes, with the right woman.

Eve said, 'You take her to bed first and I'll watch. That will break down the girl's resistance and I'll replace you after a while. I'll enjoy watching. You know women aren't really voyeuristic, to any marked extent, except in lesbian or bi-sexual affairs. I have often wondered why.'

'Because so much of it is fantasy?' I ventured.

'Perhaps,' said Eve, releasing me with a laugh, 'see you tonight then. And come dressed to kill. You are the most attractive married woman on the whole cantonment. If Karen sees a woman as lovely and sophisticated as you are, allowing another woman to handle you as I intend to do, she will assume bi-sexuality is fashionable in the grown-up world. You know that teenagers would rather die than be out of fashion.'

'Don't worry, Eve. I will dress the part I have to play. I am going to a cocktail party first, so I'll have some flying speed before I start on her. I'll try and look ultra feminine so she'll never guess that I am the same as you.'

'Are you?' she asked very gently. At that moment I found myself wondering. Eve had a peculiar magnetism I could not resist – not even in a crummy little box room in broad daylight. I put my arms around her and kissed her with a fervour which surprised me, but which Eve seemed to take for granted. I felt only that I would do anything to get this girl for her, whatever the cost. And I felt entirely willing to submit to Eve in Karen's presence, if that was what she wanted. But I struck a note of caution.

'We mustn't frighten her,' I said.

'Frighten her? Why should she be frightened? I'm a honey.'

'Well you are her Sergeant Major and three times her age. That's why.' I replied lightly. 'But for that reason, she'll enjoy it all the more once you are really in charge of her and she has relaxed. I shall watch with interest.'

Sharp at 10 o'clock that night, I turned up on her doorstep and, after a long pause, Eve let me in. I almost thought that I had come on the wrong night.

'I've nearly made her on my own,' she whispered, putting her left hand to my lips.

'So you have,' I said. 'Shall I leave you to it?'

'No, we'll stick to our original plan. I want you too. So come on in and join us.' She raised her voice. 'I am so sorry about your car, Mrs Roberts, you had better stay the night and we'll get it fixed in the morning.'

I followed Eve to her sitting room just in time to catch a glimpse of a tousled Karen buttoning up her pyjamas. I thought she looked a bit sulky. A half empty bottle of gin was on the table and two glasses, one empty. Eve immediately poured a drink for me, a large one, and another for Karen, who was slowly cheering up.

As Eve came towards me I realized she was nude underneath her négligée. She allowed it to fall slightly open as she moved. I caught my breath. This could be quite a party. Eve was a very sensuous woman in or out of uniform, but never more so than now. She looked radiant in her latent happiness. The girl had turned her on all right, I concluded.

I wondered that she should risk spoiling the intended seduction by introducing another factor. But Eve was always supremely confident in everything she did. Not for her the simple scene, she liked her sex complicated. How many young German girls had surrendered to her during her army career? She had been in the Service when German women outnumbered the men ten to one because of the casualties on the Eastern front. They would have been sitting ducks.

Eve, I concluded, was probably a very experienced woman, more than a match for little Karen – and for me, come to that. And pretty though Karen was, many of the German girls I had seen in the streets and shops of the local town would almost have matched her for looks. No wonder Eve had stayed in the army and then chosen to take up employment, after her service, in the Federal Republic. She spoke German fluently, which was one of her greatest assets in her job and her private love life.

'You can have my bed in this room Mrs Roberts,' said Eve, 'and I'll share with Karen next door. It's a double bed, so we'll have plenty of room.'

'You can call me Jane if you like,' I replied. 'I've always called you Eve.'

Eve smiled at me. She had got a very nice smile. We settled down to a quiet drinking session in which, I noticed, Karen was kept well supplied.

Eve picked up her hairbrush, and started to brush Karen's hair into some sort of order again, making her sit on a cushion between her knees.

I was beginning to feel relaxed. The order of battle, after all this was very nearly the army, was changed, but the objective remained the same. Eve was quite obviously going to seduce Karen in the other room, and I was going to be allowed to watch. After that . . . I stretched . . . after that, I expect Eve will make love to me, I thought. Karen was pretty, very pretty, but I knew Eve fancied me. I had known it for a long time.

'Jane,' Eve asked, 'would you like me to undress you and put you to bed, just for a luxury at the end of a long day?' She gave me another drink and one for Karen, who had finished hers before I had consumed mine.

'I'd love that. I haven't had a ladies' maid for years,' I smiled at Eve. We both knew what we were doing.

Eve smoothed down Karen's hair with her hand and started to brush her own dark locks. She had a short hair style, but her hair was nice and she was a good-looking woman. 'I wonder what her breasts are like?' I thought. I could just see the tops as the bent forward. I opened my coat so Karen could see the shape of mine. I have always been rather proud of my full, well-shaped bosom. I know 38 inches does not sound all that much, but, with a narrow back, it makes them quite large.

'We might as well use one brush. Our hair is going to mingle on the pillow,' said Eve, touching Karen gently as she did so. 'Mine too.' I thought, as Eve languidly got to her feet and came towards me.

'Turn round and I'll brush out your hair, too,' Eve said. She unclipped it and let it fall over my eyes, and flicked the brush through it with a firm hand.

'Fix yourself another drink, Karen,' she said as she removed my coat, unzipped my dress and unclipped the bra.

Then Eve started to fondle my naked breasts in full view of the girl. I turned my face round to be kissed. Things were going well so far, I concluded, as I stepped out of my clothes. I could feel Eve's body, smooth, hot and bare behind me as the fingers of her left hand explored between my legs.

'You've got the most beautiful breasts,' said Eve. 'They are so heavy and yet you could almost do without a bra.'

'Well, I tried it once for a bit, but after a while they felt uncomfortable. It made the men look, though. There were dotted lines everywhere!'

Eve pulled back the top of the bed.

'You don't sleep in nighties, do you? I always sleep in the nude and Karen's going to take those pyjamas off as soon as I get her into the next room.'

'Take them off here,' I suggested. 'I'd like to have a look.'

'No,' said Eve, looking at Karen rather as a stoat looks at a rabbit. 'This is going to be a private viewing. A private viewing of a private soldier by her N.C.O.!'

She laughed at her own sally, and so did Karen, who was showing all the signs of having drunk herself into a state of schoolgirl giggles. Eve went over and kissed the girl, who made no complaint as the older woman's hand was thrust into her pyjamas. As they kissed I could see, quite clearly, that Eve's fingers were right up and in the girl's vagina, and they remained like that for a full five minutes. I felt hot and open myself as I watched.

Karen's shining hair cascaded over her shoulders. How she ever made it look Army fashion for parade without a routine bun, I will never know. There was so much of it. Eve ran her hand through the girl's hair. She was a good foot taller than Karen, and she was kneeling with one leg on the sofa to bring her mouth down to the cadet's upturned and half open lips.

Suddenly, she stopped, and said, 'Do you love me?'

Karen said 'I adore you.'

'Does that mean you will give me what I want? Say it in front of Jane.'

There was a long silence.

'Go on say it.'

Karen looked up and gazed at Eve with an expression which answered the question without words.

'Say it,' said Eve. 'Say it out loud.'

Very quietly Karen said 'Yes.' I could only just hear her.

Eve opened the door of the bedroom and switched off the light in mine. Then she pushed the girl through the door with one hand in the small of the back, smacking her bottom quite hard with the other. The violence of the blow surprised me, and it certainly surprised Karen, who cried out in pain and fright.

Eve shut the door behind her and locked it.

I discovered that I had, through a well placed two-way mirror, a full view of the other room. Eve had dropped her négligée to the floor and stood nude before her sacrificial lamb – if that is the right phrase to use – willing accomplice would be more accurate. As I expected, Eve had a lovely figure; a bit too well made above the waist and a little raw-boned around the hips, if one was being critical. Her pubic hair was profuse and dark, her clitoris prominent and protruding. I thought I could see the inside of her thighs glisten just a little. With that beautiful girl in front of her there was little wonder. Eve would be all ready for her.

I thought to myself, 'I bet Karen does not know what is in store for her.' Or did she? Modern girls are pretty well clued up these days.

Eve, somewhat roughly I thought, pulled the girl's pyjama trousers off and then turned her round to face what Karen, no doubt, thought was a mirror, opening her jacket so I could get a full view. I gulped and my only reaction was acute jealousy. I wanted Karen too, and I would have been much more gentle with her. She was so young and lovely, almost dewy eyed.

Eve put her hands on Karen's stomach and then in the girl's fair pubic hair, opening the lips of her vagina, with both hands, so that I could see. Probably the slap on the bottom and the roughness were specially for my benefit.

Poor Karen, I felt rather sorry for her. Eve had

been so sweet to her up to the last second, and then came that vicious blow which really hurt her. I think the slap just meant: 'And no nonsense from you from now onwards!' It all made me feel very protective. Karen was so vulnerable.

But Eve was fully in charge. Suddenly the light went out and the scene vanished from view.

All night long I heard the squeaking of the bed springs and a whispered conversation, too low to be overheard, although it seemed to consist of questions and answers. The questions, I noticed, seemed to be demanding, and the answers submissive.

'But they would be, wouldn't they?' I concluded miserably.

I hardly slept at all. Eve had promised me I could watch. I dropped off at last, after what seemed an interminable age, to find Eve in bed with me, lying on top of me and between my open legs.

'She was wonderful,' she said. 'I went all the way with her. She's asleep now.'

'You might have let me see.' I replied. Eve kissed me, thrusting her tongue into my mouth. When we came up for air some minutes later, she said:

'I simply couldn't. I felt too guilty.'

I could feel the warmth of Eve's rather positive genitals as they probed at mine.

'I bet that made you enjoy it all the more.'

'True. But there was something that made me want to take her submission in private. She made love so beautifully and did everything I told her. But you knew, even as I was accepting what she so willingly gave me, I was planning to have you afterwards.'

Eve put one hand in my hair and dragged my head back. Then she proceeded to give me an obvious love bite on my neck. I tried to pull away but Eve persisted. John would notice it when I got home. For the rest of the week I would have to wear a scarf. Eve went on kissing me in that way until I climaxed. I could not have escaped if I had tried.

Before she went back to Karen. Eve told me all about her. Apparently, Karen had developed an obvious crush on her warden as soon as she arrived, and in bed needed no encouragement to co-operate, especially after drinking the best part of half a bottle of gin. I suspect Eve knew this all along and just wanted me as well, using Karen as bait. Women are always doing this to me I thought, as Eve went down on me. And she was an expert. She practically drew the ensuing orgasm from my willing, undulating hips. If little Karen had had the same treatment, and I knew full well she had, she was a very lucky girl – slap or no slap.

As Eve left me she said:

'You are the second officer's wife I have made love to since I left the army.'

'But I thought you only had German girlfriends, so no one would find out about you.' I replied.

'No one has found out about me. I am very discreet. But she asked for it and she got it. I'll tell you about it one day. And you asked for it, too. You have been sending vibrations to me ever since you arrived.'

In due course Karen returned to the United Kingdom but later that year, came out to live with Eve in her new flat in a German provincial town where Eve had got a new job in service welfare.

I asked Eve, when I visited them, whether Karen's sister minded.

'I don't think so,' she answered. 'Girls are very independent these days. Anyway, if there's any trouble I'll have the sister too. She is only in her late twenties and from a picture Karen showed me almost as lovely as she is.'

Eve was only half serious, but I would not have put it past her. I was putty in her hands and who can say that Karen's sister would be any different in the right place at the right time? If the circumstances were propitious and Eve had anything to do with it, the sister would follow Karen into lesbian sex. Some women are good at it and Eve was one of them. She gave me an inferiority complex when it came to sex between women, I concluded with a twinge of envy.

Lesbianism is splendid if you like it, but there is a sharp cutting edge of jealousy in affairs between women. But if it was all plain and simple sailing, it would not be such fun. And as far as I am concerned, it is fun. It always has been.

After a while, the affair came to an end, and Karen married a young German aristocrat, with the traditional Von and a small castle in Lower Saxony. Karen's elder sister came out to the wedding and stayed with Eve, and, remembering her boastful promise to have the sister too, I have always wondered what happened. As I have said,

I would not have put it past Eve, knowing her as I do. She was a most determined woman, and a professional practitioner of an art that was all her own. One day I will find out, I expect. It is not the sort of news you can put in a Christmas card, but next time we meet, Eve will tell me. She would have liked two sisters, one after the other. Her conquests are rather like scalps on a redskin's belt, or notches on a cowboy's gun. But I am glad the conquest of Jane was one of them. I enjoyed every minute of my downfall and Eve knows I did.

However, one part of the story I did hear later, and that was the saga of the first year of Eve and Karen's love affair.

Eve told to me:

'You know, I am not a sadist; when I gave little Karen that very hard slap on her satin covered bottom, it was just to sober her up. I suddenly noticed that I had given her far too much to drink, and that is why I very firmly asked her if she was going to give me what I wanted and when she was slow to reply, gave her a slap on her bottom that she will remember for a long time. When I took her pyjama trousers down, you could see the full impression of my hand in red, on her white skin. Did you notice?'

'No, I only saw her full frontal. I saw the girl was on heat when you opened her up, and I also saw she was at the point of tears,' I replied.

'Well, it was a hell of a slap I gave her. I have got a strong right arm, and Karen got it full force. There is nothing worse than going to bed with a giggling schoolgirl. I always take my love making seriously,' Eve added. 'Although I say I am not a sadist, I did actually enjoy that slap. My vagina was soaking when I dropped my négligée to the ground.'

'So I noticed!' I rejoined.

'But we had a super session after that. Karen was so anxious to do anything I wanted that I really had no cause for complaint. I think that slap turned her on, too. You know, Karen was an emotional repair job. She told me she had been raped by two young men, one of whom she thought she could trust. She had run home crying and distressed; she told no one about it and spent the rest of the month worrying about being pregnant. Happily, I think she was too immature to conceive easily, although she might have done. They both finished off inside her, apparently. However, that put her off boys completely. Her substitution was innocent affairs with other girls, and having a crush on any good-looking lady teacher in sight – a state of mind which I took full advantage of. She is the most beautiful child I have ever had nude, with her legs open, in my life. Thank heaven for those two boys!'

Karen did not need gin. She would have gone to bed with Eve stone cold sober. It was her first experience of the lesbian act with a grown woman and she was longing for it.

But Eve told me she was not going to bring her up to be exclusively lesbian and for two reasons: one, she liked very young girls, and Karen would grow up; and two, Eve was essentially promiscuous.

One girl for life was not for her, however lovely and however devoted. She once told me that some of the German girls she had had were as young as 16 or 17. She said she preferred them that age, if given a choice.

'Mind you, I had their mothers and older sisters too, but a 16-year-old girl, completely untouched by hand, is quite a thrill.' Eve loved boasting.

After a few months of lesbian love from Eve, Karen was made to have supervised cuddles on the sofa with young German men under orders from Eve. Then she would take them both to bed and, insisting on the man taking precautions she would hold the girl in her arms lying underneath her, while he had sex with her. In this way, she contended, she would gradually get her to be bi-sexual. I took this explanation with a pinch of salt. I am not at all sure about Eve not having a streak of sadism in her make-up, whatever she may say.

Karen had different men each time, and in this way, had regular sexual intercourse with dozens of men, always in Eve's arms, and always under Eve's control. After she had sent them home she would make love to the girl herself. I think she *was* a sadist.

Perhaps it worked in the end. Eve had about three years of perverse love-making with her little friend, and then married her off very suitably. I hope he is kind to her.

As I have said, I have not yet found out whether Eve had Karen's sister too. But I have a well-developed bump of curiosity and I will find out one day. That young woman spent a whole week in

Eve's flat after the wedding, I understand, and I would not give much for her chances. I know Eve intended to lay her and I cannot really see so determined a woman failing to get what she wanted when she had so openly boasted about it in advance. Sooner or later I shall hear from the lips of Eve. She is a great girl for pillow talk. I once told her she had a mind like a cesspit.

'So have you! I can turn you on just by talking to you.' 'Eve can turn me on, period,' I thought, 'and I am supposed to be butch.'

It is just what Eve would have liked, the opportunity to reveal the precise nature of her perverse sexual orientation to the elder sister in the most basic possible way, by personal demonstration.

I can read Eve's tortuous mind, for I know her well, and the only way to know a women like Eve well is to go to bed with her as I did, in a submissive state of mind.

I could have struggled harder when Eve gave me that love bite on my neck, but I decided not to struggle quite hard enough, so as to accept her mark of conquest, for that was what it was. It give her the mental and physical pleasure that an orgasm, achieved from the friction of her erect clitoris on mine, gave her. That climax, I remember, went on and on, each tremor being more intense than the last one, and each being registered in the mind of Eve as a personal triumph.

In the art of erotic pleasure the physical actions of women making love seem almost minuscule compared with their emotional and mental reactions. This is what makes lesbianism, for some women, the supreme mental pleasure, transcending all others in the intensity of its emotions. It is when society fails to understand this that it fails to understand the whole nature of sex between women, which is to them at one and the same time: beautiful and cruel, kind and selfish, gentle and rough, all pervading and deeply personal. Lesbian love is not only conquest and surrender, although it is that, it is the blending together of two female personalities in an act of love which frequently takes a long time to conclude, with the loved one being willing to sacrifice her very soul to give pleasure to her friend and satisfy her sexual demands.

Lesbian love is as old as history itself and has never been fully understood by those outside its circle. But it will be practised by women, some women, as long as the world rolls round. It has been said that man is but a developed and specialized female. If this is true, it is his very efficiency which is his undoing. His pleasure in the act of love is swiftly achieved and, for his female partner, often never. Although to be fair, some men do try very hard to be good lovers and some achieve their ambition. I am a feminist but I have never been anti-male. I just like making love to women. That does not make me antipathetic to men.

12

Chapter 12

When John's regiment returned to the United Kingdom, we were posted to the depot, situated in an industrial town in the Midlands.

At Christmas, we went to an other ranks' party which lasted into the early hours of the morning. There was a jolly and rather buxom woman there, the mother of one of the young soldiers, who went round with a piece of mistletoe, encouraging the couples to kiss. I noticed that she always ended up holding it over my head to give tacit permission for whichever soldier I was dancing with, to kiss me.

I think both John and I had too much to drink that night, because we both ended up in separate buses going back to the depot. I was in the arms of some young man who was determined to get his hand up my thighs, and the soldier's mother, although this was not her son, was beside me encouraging me to let him. Her name I found out, was Jackie, short for Jacqueline I suppose, and she assured me that my husband, in the other bus, was probably having it off with one of her teenaged daughters whom she had paired him off with. I began to get alarmed. The young soldier had got his hand where he wanted it and was petting me rather too successfully. His mouth was glued to mine and his rock-hard penis felt like a furnace on my leg. It would only be a matter of time before I was raped, especially with his old harridan aiding and abetting the act. 'I wouldn't put it past her to hold me down,' I thought in a panic.

As soon as I could get my mouth from his for a second, I said, 'Please help me, I don't want to go too far with this young soldier.'

Jackie said, 'Would you prefer me instead? I have lesbian tendencies, and they'll keep off you if you come with me. Everyone knows what I'm like!'

'Yes,' I said with great relief. I did not fancy Jackie. She was the last woman I would have chosen, but here was safety. Safety in the arms of a woman with thighs like tree trunks, a large and pendulous bosom, which not even her bra could fully support or conceal, and hands like a manual labourer. She was a manual labourer actually, I subsequently discovered she worked in a local laundry, cleaning carpets.

Her only redeeming features were large brown eyes and coarse, shoulder length, brown hair.

She removed my ardent suitor with one movement of her arm, and substituted her own body with equal dexterity. She put her mouth onto mine, and her tongue was inside, almost as our lips met. She was a lesbian all right, a rather unattractive one, and as butch as they make them, but there was no doubt what was going to happen to me now. But that was better than being made pregnant by one of my husband's soldiers. 'To hell with John,' I thought 'why did he want to get drunk at a time like this?'

Jackie was being very persistent. 'We'll be home in a minute,' she told me, 'and if you come up to my room I'll fuck you instead of letting one of the boys do so. Otherwise there will be a gang-bang and you will be their target for the night.'

I willingly accepted her offer. But I would have a word with John in the morning. He had got me into this situation. I wondered what he was doing. Fast asleep or locked in the arms of one of Jackie's daughters? What a mess!

About six soldiers got off the bus with us, and two or three girls, either Jackie's daughters or their friends. I hurriedly followed Jackie to her room and heard her lock the door behind us. She put the key on the dressing table and my watch, earrings and handbag as she swiftly and expertly undressed me.

Then she removed her own clothes.

Her huge breasts sagged to her navel and her mass of black pubic hair looked like a forest. She put her arms around me and, lifting up one of her breasts, she invited me to put the long, hardened teat in my mouth.

As I did so she told me in a contemptuous tone of voice I had never heard before, as harsh as an iron rasp, to take down my pants and tights, my last remaining vestige of clothing. I lowered them down to my ankles and stepped out of them, sucking obediently at the large, rough teat, which almost filled my mouth.

Jackie grabbed hold of my hair and wrapped it round her hand, then quite deliberately and sensuously she rubbed her thick, curling pubic hair in mine. Suddenly I felt her swollen clitoris touch me. It was like an electric shock. She prised my legs apart and thrust herself between them. She moved like a man and with equal strength.

Despite my initial physical revulsion for the woman, my vagina, I knew, was hot and wide open. It had been for some time, I realized to my chagrin. Fancy being sexually excited by a rough woman like this! I didn't think I'd ever had a more unattractive nipple in my mouth. And as for Jackie's breasts, I could barely lift them they were so heavy.

'Jane,' I told myself, 'you've sunk pretty low to give yourself to a woman you wouldn't normally even glance at in the street.'

Jackie was not even wearing any scent. Her naked body smelt hot, sweaty and very female. I noticed she did not shave under her arms. There were great protruding tufts of hair.

I found myself thrust back on to the bed, and was enveloped by female flesh. Her clitoris was half inside me by now and despite myself I began to find her great breast exciting. She insisted I sucked it, holding me to it by the grip of her fist in my hair.

Suddenly a key turned in the lock and the door opened. In a second a soldier, nude as the day he was born, was in bed beside us.

Jackie pretended to thrust him off but I suspected it had all been arranged. For some time she allowed him to rub himself off up and down my leg. I ignored the young man and concentrated on giving the woman the pleasure she had demanded, thereby hoping to gain her continued protection.

Then, to my dismay, she turned me on my side, with my bottom towards the soldier – I did not even know which one he was – and I felt his hand inside me, and his penis, thick and hard against my back. Jackie had my legs wide open, with her own massive thighs between them. My hair was twisted, so it hurt, around her large, muscular hands. She had both her hands in my hair now, and the message was plain, 'Do as I tell you.' I think she was enjoying the pain she was deliberately inflicting.

Despite my fear of pregnancy, or of being unfaithful to my husband with a man, I was finding the attractions of Horse, as I heard the woman call him, not unpleasant. In fact, I am ashamed to say, I was becoming very excited, physically.

The drink, the petting, the grossness of the great butch dyke who was handling me as if she owned me – perhaps she did at that moment – and the ardour of the young man and his hard, thick penis, all contributed to my state of mind, which was near to surrendering. Not that it mattered much what my state of mind was. This was a threesome, stage-managed by a very strong and determined woman. Her nipple touched the back of my throat and the grip of her two hands in my freshly washed and silky hair never relaxed.

'My hair won't look freshly washed and silky tomorrow,' I thought. I had noticed earlier in the evening, with distaste, how coarse and dirty her hands were. They were like her body, unwashed. And yet, she was exciting me. Or was it the young man? I was too confused to work it out. I only knew that the great rigid penis now moving up and down between my legs, was shortly going to thrust itself inside me and, with Jackie prising my legs as far apart as she could get them, there was nothing I could do about it. Nothing? Then I realized that I did not want to do anything about it. I was enjoying myself, despite everything.

A few minutes later he was inside me, inside and right up to the hilt in my body, and he went to work manfully. A private soldier and an officer's wife. It had to be good, and he was enjoying it too. So was I, but I found myself torn between the pleasure of his thrusts and the touch of Jackie's clitoris on mine. Never for one moment did she relax the grip in my hair, and her nipple seemed to fill my mouth as I sucked it like a child.

Then I climaxed. It was like a warm, trembling wave of passion. I cried out with pleasure. The last thing I wanted to do, in this young soldier's arms was betray myself like this. He was not to know that it was Jackie and the smell of her hot, female body I was climaxing over. He would think it was him and his male skill.

Anyway, whatever he thought, he gave a few more hard thrusts and ejaculated inside me. I could feel it and the increasing ease with which his large penis moved in and out of me. He had seemed to stretch me wide with his first lunge, and his last half dozen went in and out on the lubrication of my own juices and his ejaculation, with the ease of conquest. But I was Jackie's conquest not his, and she knew it. She climaxed, too before she released my hair and let me remove my mouth from her breast. Her nipple was wet with my saliva and my teeth marks showed around its base. In my passion I must have bitten deep, but her nipple was too tough to register any pain. At least, Jackie never showed any reaction to my bite. Her breast had been suckled by so many children that it was just about impervious to anything I could do to it.

I never even saw the young soldier. He withdrew and went out without a word to say for himself, and I spent the rest of the night with his mother. For the young man was her son, and I was not the first girl she had procured for 'Horse,' whose real name was Bill, she told me later. She got a kick out of it she said: 'Especially when it's an officer's wife.'

Jackie made love to me two or three times more during the night. I woke up to find her licking me out, and I climaxed half in my sleep. Perhaps that was why I never got pregnant. Jackie made such a thorough job of it.

When my husband and I met the next evening we were rather quiet. I think we were both a bit ashamed of ourselves. It was a sexual escapade which, for once, we did not discuss. Candid confessions were not the order of the day and I have never found out who he slept with, although I could hazard a guess. One of Jackie's daughters came home with the milk, looking as if she had been pulled through a hedge backwards.

'You been sleeping with Mum?' she said with a giggle. 'Well I know what's happened to you.'

'You go and wash your mouth out with soap girl!' retorted Jackie.

And to me, 'Don't take any notice of her.' Fiona was her name, a fresh and fairhaired 18-year-old, used as bait by Jackie to get me on my own and away from the protection of my well-wined husband. And she looked as if she had enjoyed the whole thing. I wondered if John had enjoyed her. A pang of jealousy caused my heart to beat more quickly.

Although I never knew for certain if it was Fiona, she would do for first suspect. I smiled at her and asked her if she would like a job driving for me.

'Oh yes, thanks, I love driving.' Her blue eyes were bright with interest.

'Well come and see me tomorrow and I'll start you at the usual salary,' I told her. I had plans for little Fiona. At one stroke I would revenge myself in the nicest possible way, and pay off both John and Jackie.

I narrowed my eyes and looked at her, still smiling. Yes, I'll make her, I said to myself. And I'm not often wrong. Fiona was as good as conquered. I had made up my mind about that.

To her mother I said: 'Thank you for looking after me last night. I'll never forget your kindness.'

I let Jackie kiss me on the mouth in front of her daughter, and she made quite a job of it, tongue included.

'A small taste of what is in store for you, darling,' I thought, with Fiona in mind.

Back home I told John I had engaged a girl called Fiona to drive for me. I thought I saw him start, but he just said, without looking up. 'Oh, that will be nice.' He was so relaxed, I felt perhaps I had misjudged him. But I was determined to proceed as if my first hunch was the right one. It would be more fun that way. And anyway, I had a debt to pay her mother, had I not?

Sharp at 9 o'clock on the morrow, Fiona arrived, and I took her out in the car to a network of quiet country roads and found her to be a competent driver. She had passed her test first time, and was pleased that I found her satisfactory.

But it was not just for driving I had engaged her. In order to ingratiate myself with her, I had her drive to the nearest good shopping centre and there bought her a whole new outfit of clothes right down to bras and panties. It gave me a good chance to look at her too. She really had a delightful figure, and I was able to see her bare breasts as she changed from bra to bra, and a glimpse of her fair pubic hair as she stepped out of her pants. Then, with a bottle of expensive French scent to complete the day we went off to lunch.

Fiona looked radiant, and she was obviously going to enjoy working for me. She was going to live in, and her bedroom was down the end of the passage, about 10 yards from ours. I was not worried about John. He was the perfect example of a faithful husband normally, and if this little minx had not been set on him by her mother, would have remained so.

I always tell John everything. He is regaled with every detail of what I do with women but I rarely let him watch. I do not like being watched, very few lesbians do, except sometimes by another woman. But this time I planned to make an exception. When I had got her completely under my thumb – and that was not for a while yet – John was going to be allowed to watch his adorable little Fiona giving herself to a woman. I had a feeling Fiona was not going to like that, but that is why she was not going to be asked, she was going to be told.

Fiona knew all about her mother, who was notorious in the town. She told me she had even made love to one of her own daughters, Pamela, the eldest one, from the age of 16. 'She kissed me once, full on the mouth, with her tongue inside. But I refused to respond.'

Then she said 'You slept with Mum. Are you like her?'

'Yes,' I said quietly, 'but I can quite understand that you wouldn't want to make love with your own relation.'

We left it at that for the while, but a few days later I took her gently in my arms and kissed her. In a few minutes I knew I was on to a winner. This child would not give me any trouble. Fiona was mine.

That night I slipped into her bed and made love to her. Fiona was asleep when I arrived, and I had my hand on her naked breast before she woke up.

'Oh, it's you Jane, is it?' she mumbled sleepily.

'Yes pet, it's me,' I replied 'and I've come to thank you for coming to live with me.'

I petted her for a while and then went down on her and brought her on a bit with my tongue. She climaxed, and was asleep almost as soon as the last sigh. I went to sleep too, just where I was, and only left her as the light started to steal through the curtains to herald a new day.

John made love to me when I finally returned to our bed. My fingers and my report on the state of little Fiona were quite enough to turn him on. I did not tell him what I had in store for him. Fiona and I were going to provide him with quite an exhibition when the time was ripe. I do not know what made me want to expose Fiona to this, but there it is. Perhaps it was her mother. I am sure it was her mother!

For nearly a year Fiona and I had a deep physical and mental relationship. She was bi-sexual, rather than lesbian, but she did not seem to hanker after a boy. I seemed to satisfy her every need; financial, emotional and sexual.

One evening in the drawing room, I pulled her to me on the sofa and kissed her on the mouth in front of John. I saw him get hard as I did so, but I noticed Fiona was disturbed by it. I ignored her feelings completely and put my hand on her breast. Fiona removed it and I put it back. This time she accepted it and I went on to a full petting session, including putting my hand up her skirt – all in the full view of my husband, whom I allowed to see everything. I even opened her up with my fingers so he could look inside.

Then I stood her up and said: 'We are going to bed. You can come too if you like, John.'

I undressed Fiona and myself and locked her in my arms on the marriage bed. John sat, fully dressed, in a chair. I gave her the full works, finally going down on her and making her put her finger on her clitoris as I licked her out. She climaxed in my mouth and I slid up her body to kiss her on the mouth. I like letting a girl taste herself on my lips. It reminds them of what has just happened.

John was on his feet, his penis out, thick, strong and rampant. Someone was going to get it and I decided it was going to be Fiona.

Beckoning John, I turned her face towards him, and let him masturbate in her face. Just before he ejaculated, I encouraged her to take the swollen knob between her lips. I saw her throat working as she swallowed obediently. With my fingers I squeezed the last drop out for her.

Then I am afraid, I sent her back to her own bed. Faithful though he might be, an 18-year-old girl – she was nearly 19 now that I come to think of it – might have been too much of a temptation. I am a jealous wife where my husband and other women are concerned. And I expect him to be jealous where men are concerned. My little girls are another matter. They are entirely my concern as long as I tell John all about it afterwards. And I do.

One night I decided to take Fiona to a night club. I put on my black trouser suit and made her wear a pretty evening frock. She had her hair done simply, with just a parting at the side, and over one eye. A very young, schoolgirl style. My hair was swept severely up.

When we got to the Seven Veils, as the place was called, I led Fiona in with one hand on the back of her neck. It was dark inside but, when her eyes got used to the concealed lighting, Fiona saw that the place was frequented only by women. There were butch lesbians everywhere, and a few little faded femmes.

We ordered drinks from the waitress and while they were coming I turned and kissed Fiona for a full five minutes, with one hand very obviously cupping her breast. There was a muffled cheer from the audience as I removed my mouth from hers. I do not know if Fiona was blushing, the light was too poor to see.

Eventually an old butch dyke called Big Billie turned up and sat down without invitation.

'Where did you kidnap her from?' she said.

'From the local secondary school,' I replied. 'She's doing her "O" levels next term.'

I laid it on a bit thick. But in that light it was easily believable. Fiona looked not a bit over 15.

'Would you like to dance, honey?' said Billie, leading her off without waiting for a reply.

'You don't mind, do you?' she called over her shoulder to me.

I caught sight of them once or twice, and the second time I noticed Billie had her hand inside Fiona's dress, handling her small breasts.

'Dirty old bag,' I thought, 'fancy doing that to what she thinks is a fifteen year old schoolgirl!'

Then they vanished. After an hour I went to look for them and found them in a bedroom on the upper floor. I had taken girls there in the past and

I knew just where to stand so I could watch, unseen. This is what I had planned.

Billie had her supposed schoolgirl, naked on a bed with her, and on the table beside the bed was a 6-inch dildo with a massive knob and straps to mount it. It was black and obscene in its appearance.

I waited in the wings and eventually Billie rose from the girl's body, and strapped on the dildo. Gently she inserted it into Fiona, then proceeded to have sexual intercourse with her in a far from gentle fashion, grasping her fair hair in her hand and bending Fiona back over the edge of the bed.

She must have done it fairly skilfully because I heard Fiona climax most satisfactorily. Even though Billie's mouth was clamped to hers, you could have heard it in the next street.

I tiptoed away. Eventually Billie brought Fiona back, suspiciously rebrushed and combed.

'We decided to sit that dance out,' explained Fiona.

'You want to look after her,' said Billie. 'She'll be taking her "A" levels otherwise. She's had a good teacher, of course.'

I took Fiona home, but things were never quite the same after that. I do not like dildos. Some girls do, and Fiona was one of them. Eventually she went with Billie and became her little femme in a nightclub they opened jointly, somewhere in Spain. I expect she gets that black dildo every other night, because she has never looked back since then. And her mother goes out to stay with them. So she must approve.

I get a Christmas card every year. But that's life. There's not much virtue in quantity. I prefer quality and if one door closes another opens. I have always thought that it is the very first time you make it with a girl that is the best. The second time is just a repetition of the first.

But then, at that point in my life I had never fallen in love with a woman. They were just conquests for me. I suppose it was only the equivalent of a man 'sowing his wild oats', as they call it, and then settling down with one woman for the rest of his life.

For that was what was to happen to me. And I found her in the most unexpected place, the boardroom of a public company. It was love at first sight, and it was Elizabeth, aged 20, who turned a sordid little history into a love story. A lesbian love story, but a love story just the same.

But first, for one brief interlude, I returned to my old haunts, the highways and byways of sexual promiscuity. I desperately wanted to find and fall in love with the perfect girl. Only then would I feel that the licence allowed me by my husband was justified. To tell the truth, I was beginning not to admire myself greatly. Self-deprecation is all very well but, after a while, it tends to destroy one's basic morale. Lesbians have their standards like everyone else. Perhaps I was taking myself too seriously or perhaps I was clutching to myself 'that tiny rag, my last shred of honour'. Whatever it was, my ultimate salvation was not yet to be. I had a date with time. And, until I kept it, my salvation had to wait.

❧13❧

Chapter 13

It was once said that you eventually meet everyone you know, but have not seen for a long time, in London's Piccadilly Circus. And so it was with me. I had just come to town to buy some new shoes and a hat for a fashionable wedding to which we had been asked, when I ran into my old friend and co-conspirator, Eve. She greeted me like a long lost cousin and all thoughts of new shoes and hats vanished as we slid into the nearest pub. My first question was:

'What are you doing now?'

'I am working with the Federal Forestry Commission on the effects of acid rain on the trees and lakes of Western Europe', she replied. She handed me a glass of Pimms Number One, which she knew I was fond of, especially when it was made properly with ice, cucumber, mint, cherries and banana – all the rubbish as we used to say when we were very young and wanted real alcohol, and our parents had organized it otherwise. It was a hot day and I was very ready for a long, cool drink.

'Heavens, you change your jobs just about as often as your girlfriends,' was all I could think of saying.

'Oh no, I am going steady now. Would you like to meet her?'

I looked at Eve. She was as lovely as my last memory of her, and as sure of herself as she ever was.

'I would indeed. Are you very much in love with her?'

'Very,' said Eve. 'And I thought I would never get hooked. I used to think I needed a change once a week. Come on, finish your drink and we'll go to my hotel. It's just a stone's throw from here.'

We wandered off, pleased to be in each other's company again. I suppose we would not, in ordinary circumstances have been such bosom friends, but there is a great unifying bond in having the same sexual defect, if it is a defect. Personally, if there were a medical cure for lesbianism readily available, I do not think the queue for treatment would be a very long one, and whether it was long or short you would not find me in it. Nor, I suspect would you find Eve.

The hotel to which we repaired was one which had been a favourite resort of American servicemen and English girls in World War Two. Some wit said that a couple of divisions of Anglo-American troops had been fathered under its extensive roof. Anyway, that is what my mother told me they used to say. I never dared to ask her if she had any

Yankee boyfriends, but I expect she did. Most girls did during the war, I think. And I really do not blame them. After all, most of their boys were away and you have got to do something to keep yourself amused. Not all girls are as easily satisfied with their own sex as I am.

I found myself wondering if any of the United States service women were of our persuasion and concluded that one or two of them must have been. I had seen some simply beautiful young American women in uniform in Germany, and I mentally reserved the subject for discussion with Eve. She would know, if anyone did.

We entered the foyer of the hotel and Eve, after collecting her key, took me straight up to her room. There, sitting at the dressing table powdering her nose, was a girl I had never seen before, but who nevertheless seemed familiar, as Eve went up and kissed her.

'This, Jane, is Penelope, Penny to her friends, and she is Karen's sister. Jane was a friend of Karen's,' she added, as a word of explanation.

Eve kissed Penny again, this time on the mouth and for a full half minute. Eve was always showing off, I thought. Penny's face was scarlet at being kissed like that in front of another woman. But that did not save her.

'Don't worry darling,' said Eve, 'she's one of us.'

Penny was so like her sister that my recognition of her was immediate. Up to that moment I had not even known her name, but she was our little friend's sister all right and, on balance, even more lovely. She was slim and high-breasted with a bee-stung mouth like Karen's, and eyes which were an even brighter blue. Her hair was blonde and as fine as silk. As Eve ran her fingers through it, it fell away from her touch like sand in an hour glass. It was so fine it almost slipped in her hand. Eve held up a stray lock for me to see and then dropped it. Penny was still blushing at being displayed as if she were a prize cage bird at a show.

I had a feeling at that moment, that I was going to see more of Penny before the day was out. Having let me see Karen as I had, the elder sister was unlikely to fare any better, even if Eve was in love with her. Eve treated the objects of her love with high handed authoritarianism. Democratic love-making was for others. Marriage to Eve, and that is how Eve and Penny saw their love life, was a sort of one party state.

I heard the story later. After the wedding reception given by Eve in one of those people's community halls the Germans do so efficiently, Penny found herself in the arms of a rather pushy young soldier who had done well on the champagne. Agreeing to accompany him to his car, to sit the next dance out as he put it, she was very nearly raped. Eve it was who rescued her and took her back to the flat, where she comforted the girl only too successfully.

If anything, Penny was more sexy than Karen, and more bi-sexually orientated. Karen's feeling for women was induced by her mini gang-bang, but the elder sister was a natural. She fell in love that night, so deeply in love that not even a detailed account of her sister's sex life in Germany was enough to dent the shining armour of her passion for Eve.

'I am sure you were very kind to her, and she was lucky to find such a nice friend,' was her only reaction.

Eve told me that although Penny was 14 years older than Karen, they were both very similar in bed. They even tended to smell and taste like each other, she said. And Eve had tasted both sisters very thoroughly so she should know. I was only surprised she had not had both of them in bed together. 'Perhaps she will one day', I thought. That would be Eve all over.

I cancelled all my plans and told John on the telephone that I was staying in London for the night. He was most intrigued to hear that I had met Eve again. My husband trusts me as I trust him. My indiscretions with women do not count, and he knows I would never betray him with a man. That is why we have such a happy marriage, and when I get back from each petty encounter, he listens to every word I tell him, and takes me in his arms and loves me all the more because of it. Infidelity would count, but indiscretions do not, that is how he sees it. If I tried to go straight tomorrow, and I could not do that now, however hard I tried, the sun would go behind a cloud for him. He enjoys my other sex life as much as I do. It quite simply turns him on as nothing else can. I have often wondered how he would have fared if he had married an ordinary run-of-the-mill girl. I think he would have found it rather dull.

The hotel arranged a room for me without any

difficulty. I was lucky, seeing it was the height of the season, and it proved a very useful place in which to hang up my coat, because that is the only use I made of it. I spent the night, of course, with Eve and Penny.

I made love to Penny with Eve lying beside her, her lips to her cheek or in her hair, and her hand forever down round our genitals, touching and joining us together as she felt was best. What I was never allowed to do to the little sister, whom Eve had used merely as an instrument of her pleasure, I was encouraged and aided to do with the one she really loved. However, I did not bother to moralize about it all. I took what was offered and enjoyed it. And so did Penny. Being sort of prostituted, although not for money, by her female lover excited her in just the same way that I had noticed with other girls.

Some women like being treated badly, and I treated Penny badly. I did everything to her it is possible for a woman to do to another girl in bed, including for the first and only time, the use of a modern, high technology double dildo. This was at Eve's behest. She strapped it on to me, switched on the built-in, battery-operated, vibrator and guided it in. It had a rather large knob and was short and thick, which was a good thing really. I used it with such vigour that I might have hurt her had it been too long. Poor Penny climaxed ecstatically. She looked so beautiful as she reached the critical moment, lying there in the arms of two women, both of whom were enjoying her personal surrender to pleasure in ultra-feminine abandon. I can remember thinking:

'This ought to be on TV. What a wonderful video it would make!' I get thoughts like that at times.

Later on, Eve took her too, as I watched. I then came to the conclusion that I had actually been rather gentle, as the girl accepted everything from her lover with a reaction that was almost akin to gratitude. And as she climaxed, Penny turned her face to mine on the orders of Eve, and we kissed. It was a subtle touch, and it was the sort of thing I had arranged myself on occasions, so I followed the reasoning.

I can remember thinking that it was the wettest kiss I had ever had from a girl. She had probably filled her mouth with saliva, or else Eve had. I did not care which it was, they were both attractive women and at that moment in time I loved them both equally. As I was kissing Penny, Eve gripped my hair in her clenched fist to hold me there. It was only symbolic. I needed no holding, but the gesture excited me. I had one of Penny's legs gripped between mine, and I climaxed at almost the same time as she did. I think that pleased Eve. She felt she had had us both and, in a manner of speaking, I suppose she had.

Penny enjoyed every bit of it and especially the rough bits. She was as delicate as a little Dresden doll, and yet she seemed to thrive on what we did to her. Personally, that particular scene is not for me, and of my own volition, I would never have embarked upon it. Why? Because an artificial aid is not part of me, it is a foreign body in the act of love, and I can manage quite well in my own way, in my own time. And although I can be dominant, and have been, on balance I prefer to be gentle and just love the girl I am with. But you have to try it both ways to know how you really are, I suppose.

On the subject of sex aids, my husband once told me that a brother officer of his got hold of a catalogue full of pictures of them, and someone in the Mess said:

'Yes, some of them are so good, you don't even have to have a woman!'

As far as I am concerned, and I know now for sure, they are absolutely out. Eve was the sort of woman who had to try everything, but even she will find that there is no substitute for love and cuddles between women, as I have found out by trial and error.

Nevertheless, I asked Eve if she would like both sisters in bed together, and she said:

'It is my very firm intention to arrange that. I've already told Penny and she's game, although I think she will only do it to please me. However, once I get them both in the same bed, I'll make them want to do it for other reasons.'

Before we parted Eve took us both to a concert at the Albert Hall. We all liked classical music, and we had had enough of love making for a while, especially Penny.

The first part of the concert was devoted to the works of Tchaikovsky, and performed by a well-known metropolitan philharmonic orchestra. We heard the '1812 Overture', which is rather noisy, but as a soldier's wife and daughter, I have always rather liked it. Then we had Mussorgsky's 'A Night on a Bare Mountain' – great stuff, and just what we three deserved after our night of wickedness. Then finally, we listened to Wagner's Prelude to Act III of 'Lohengrin'. I had heard the works of this famous composer a lot in Germany, and almost knew this one by heart.

I gathered from Penny that they often went to concerts. There are so many good orchestras in London that you could go to a different one every night if you had a mind to. So Eve and Penny had two things in common, the love of good classical music and a little sister in Lower Saxony, waiting in the wings for her call. And when it comes, Eve will have them both, and she will encourage them to make love to each other in an act of sheer lesbian incest. In my vivid imagination, during Wagner's music, I could see the younger sister's long, rich hair spread over the pillow and Penny's silky, shorter, fair hair, half covering her face as they embraced under Eve's expert tutelage. Poor Karen, she would be so pleased to be back where she always wanted to stay. Perhaps I should not be too sorry for her. She had always been willing to do anything to get Eve. And Eve had always been willing to make her do it. There would be nothing faked that night. When Penny had her orgasm, it would be the beauty of her younger sister's hair in her hands that triggered it off. And with Karen – well Eve would think of something for her! Eve has what the army calls power of command. I prefer to call it a sort of hypnotic ascendancy over other women in bed, but a rose by any other name would smell as sweet. I wondered if Karen's husband would ever get his wife back. I hoped so, I rather liked him.

Eve told me the sequel when we met for drinks in the West End, before she went on to an old comrades' reunion dinner. She was a split personality really, none of her old friends in the army even guessed at her secret inclinations. She was widely regarded as a most moral person, not even vaguely interested in sex, let alone our sort of sex. Eve had a good brain and was possessed of an almost masculine insight into military affairs. She would have made a good general officer if women had ever been allowed to rise to overall command. To be fair to the army, Eve refused to be considered for a commission when offered one. She earned more money as a Senior N.C.O. with no overheads, she told me, and she had easier access to the young women under her command, although she had never been known to take advantage of the fact. I think she just liked to be near them and to fantasize about them whenever she felt like it.

'Often, as I have been giving a lecture, I have mentally, taken the young girl private soldier to bed and put her clothes back on again before my closing remarks,' she once said to me, quite seriously.

There was an orchestra playing in the lounge where we were having our drinks. They played Sibelius' Symphony No. 1 and then Finlandia.

Eve said, a propos of nothing, but then she was never far off the subjct when she was with me:

'Isn't it funny that our prediliction has always been social death, if known, but it has never, ever been illegal.'

'Yes, and that's why we keep it as an invisible web, known only to ourselves. I was told the reason it has never been illegal was because no minister could be found brave enough to take the Bill to Queen Victoria for the Royal Assent.' I replied.

Curiously enough, neither Eve nor I really approve of male homosexuality. We acknowledge it exists, but we feel it is much more unnatural than lesbianism.

'It is a denial of manhood,' Eve once said disapprovingly. 'Whereas when two women make love they are still feminine.'

I am feminine, I know, but I have sometimes wondered, when Eve puts on a dildo how feminine she feels? It is just pretending to be a man and a pale imitation of a man at that. That is why I do not warm to them very much, whether they are high technology or the old-fashioned ones.

When I make love to a girl I am still a woman and very much so. I never think of myself as other than feminine and the joy of lesbianism, to use the with-it phrase, is contained in the one single thought that I am as completely female as the girl in my arms.

One of my cousins once said:

'Both sexes are soft on homosexuality in the opposite sex.' Well. I am not. I practise one and condemn the other. There is no justice in this stance

I know, and I am truly sorry, but that is how I feel and so do most non-political lesbians.

'Tell me about Karen,' I said.

'All right, but come up to my room. We have three hours before I have got to be there, and we can't talk here.'

We drifted upstairs. Eve shut and locked the door and turned to me with a determined look on her face.

'Come to bed,' she demanded. 'I'll tell you there.'

We undressed and slid beneath the sheets. Eve kissed me. We were back in our old relationship, breast to breast and mouth to mouth.

'Aren't you being unfaithful to Penny?' I asked.

'Yes,' said Eve, 'but she can't and I can.' A rather male attitude I thought. Was she so feminine?'

Eve had her hand on my vulva. I opened my legs, willingly, to receive her soft and questing fingers.

'Tell me,' I said. 'I want to know.'

I kissed her back in the way I knew she liked. I was wet and wide open already and Eve's hand was half inside me, her fingers very gently manipulating my clitoris. I put my arm around her and played wth her soft, dark hair, in what I hoped was a fairly seductive way. I liked her hair and I would have liked it longer, but it would not have suited her.

'Well,' said Eve, 'we met Karen at Heathrow and she was so pleased to see us. She looked radiant and as pretty as ever. We drove her back to our flat and I took them both to bed that night.'

'You are pretty ruthless.' I thought, but all I said was:

'I knew nothing would stop you, not even the natural reluctance of two sisters.'

'They were not reluctant really, you know, under my control their pleasure was completely genuine. They had probably wanted to do it for years but were too inhibited to break the ultimate social taboo. I helped them to cross the blood knot! I enjoyed that night. I made them do it. I made them want to do it.'

'I am sure you enjoyed it.' I replied. 'That's why I love you, Eve. You stop at nothing once you have made up your mind. I hope you were kind to them. You were always kind to me, almost always.' I concluded, thinking about the love bite.

I remember, too, John getting so excited, when he made love to me the next night, that I was quite sore in the morning. It was the love bite on my neck, inflicted by the mouth of a woman, while she was having sexual relations with me, that turned him on. I had never seen him so aroused and I was quite pleased it excited him, because I love my husband equally with my girl friends. They are just two sides to a golden coin, minted I trust, in Elysium, the Fields of the Blessed in Grecian mythology, because I have never felt the slightest twinge of guilt about my love life, other than for my excessive promiscuity.

Well, it seems Eve took them both to her king-sized bed and made love to them each in turn, with the lights full on and then, in the darkness of the night, later on, she induced Penny to pet Karen and then to go down on her. This was Eve's little triumph but as to whether the girl was thinking of her sister or Eve, at the moment of climax, seems to me about as important as to how many angels can dance on the point of a needle.

As she was telling me all this Eve was petting me very successfully. She has always been able to excite me and I never feel butch when I am in her arms.

I said to Eve:

'Are you going to keep Karen with you now?'

'No,' she replied. 'I expect I could if I tried, but I am not in the business of breaking up happy marriages and she is very happily married. They are going to start a family next year. No, Penny is my girl. I just wanted to see if I could make two sisters make love to each other. It was quite easy in the event, and they enjoyed it as much as I think they got pleasure from watching me with the other. While I was kissing Karen, I slipped my hand under the sheets, to find Penny had her hand between her legs stimulating herself, as she saw what I was doing to her younger sister. So she, for one, did not disapprove, or if she did, her libido was stronger than her disapproval. When I made love to Penny, when we were alone, the night after Karen left, she was more sexually excited than usual. I shall not do it again, but just for once, two sisters, doing my bidding in bed, is a scene to remember. Especially, as they were both so beautiful.

Eve was as good as her word. Like me, she was tired of flitting around and wanted a satisfying love affair instead, and because she had never looked at a man, it had to be a girl. I wish them well and I hope they never part. It would break Penny's heart if Eve ever left her and she and Karen are both sweet young women, well deserving happiness.

❧14❧

Chapter 14

As soon as I entered the room I saw Elizabeth. She was taking notes, her brown hair, shoulder length, straight, fine and shiny, falling over her eyes. She looked up as I entered and my heart missed a beat. She was so beautiful; I had to get to know her. This was the girl of a lifetime.

The meeting dragged on. I never heard a word. I was just gazing at my girl, whose name I did not even know.

She stood up and handed a slip of paper to the chairman, and I saw how slim and small-breasted she was. The 50-year-old chairman was a woman who looked butch to me. My years of experience did not betray me, she was butch and Elizabeth, her secretary, was also her girlfriend. All this I discovered from a friend of mine sitting at the back of the room, with whom I conferred at the end of the meeting.

Elizabeth and I met briefly and her conversation merely confirmed my attitude. She was intelligent and good-humoured as well as pretty.

After that, my interest in the affairs of this particular company, in which John was quite a large shareholder, increased in direct proportion to my ability to get to know Elizabeth. I fell in love with her long before our first social meeting, some weeks later, and my thoughts were only preoccupied with plans to take her from this woman. Elaine was her name, which was too feminine a name for so mannish a female. Elaine ordered Elizabeth around like a dog, I noticed, and in love with her as I was, the thought of that iron grey head being on the same pillow as my beloved Elizabeth, filled me with something like jealous hate.

The day came when Elizabeth accepted my invitation to tea. To avoid Elaine knowing, she had to arrange an appointment with her hairdresser.

'Don't have any cut off. It's so pretty.' I urged.

'I'll only have half an inch off, just to show willing,' she replied, with a smile.

'And don't have it shampooed and set. I'll do it for you at home. Then you will go back with it looking as if you have spent the whole afternoon at the hairdressers, and it will give us more time together.'

I waited for Elizabeth outside the salon, and she came out, five minutes later, looking much the same as when she went in. She had not had much off. She had listened to me, I thought.

She told me later, years later, that she knew what I was from the start.

'How?' I asked, 'I don't look like one, except on very special occasions, and that wasn't one of them.'

'Instinct and experience,' she replied and tossed her brown hair in the way she knew I liked.

But that time was to come. I drove her home feeling nervous and happy. I had got the girl I wanted, but how to secure her?

We had iced drinks, not tea, and after a while I said, 'Let's go upstairs and I'll wash your hair. It doesn't look as if it needs it, but it had better look freshly set.'

When we got into the bathroom she took off her dress and knelt down by the bath, where there was a convenient shower attachment. I knelt behind her and, for the first time ever, buried my face in her soft, scented, falling hair. It was heaven.

'Your hair smells nice,' I said, turning on the water and putting my hand under the tap.

'Oh, it's not warm yet. Let's go and lie on the bed while we wait.'

To my delight and relief she agreed, and it was not very long before I turned her round and kissed her. We were both in our underclothes, under the cover. It was a warm sunny afternoon, with the front door locked, and the curtains drawn.

Then I discovered something. Elizabeth's thighs and bottom were covered with whip marks.

Tearfully, she told me that it was her own fault. She was a masochist, and it was the sadism in Elaine which first attracted her to her.

'But it has got worse and worse. In the beginning it was only little taps. Now she really means it and is never satisfied until she has made me cry.'

I was outraged. And the more the story unfolded, the more protective I became. We made love that afternoon. All the way. And I made her promise to leave and come to me.

'I'll look after you for ever,' I promised. 'And I'll love you for ever. I've got a husband, but he won't interfere.'

Then, feeling weak with requited passion, I took her into the bathroom, washed and set her adorable hair, making love to her again as I did it.

'If I come to you you'll have to promise not to beat me. But you'll have to handle me firmly. I like the thought of being masochistic with a woman. It's the actual blows that upset me. Especially when they get harder everytime. I think if I stay on with Elaine she'll kill me in the end. I mean, there's a limit to endurance.'

I had to let her go back. And, knowing as I did that Elaine would probably take her that night, it was sheer agony lying at home thinking about it.

Jealousy by woman about women is sharper and deeper than heterosexual jealousy. That night I felt my heart was breaking waiting for Elizabeth who, I found out later, was being beaten at that very moment with a riding crop and was lying, in tears, on her bedroom floor. Elaine, wearing a dildo strapped to her stomach, was standing over her, dominant to the end.

Then Elaine, mounting her from behind, with neither gentleness nor pity, had my beloved Elizabeth, sobbing her heart out, for the very last time.

After she was finished, Elizabeth had to kneel in front of her and kiss her, saying she was sorry she had gone out to see another woman without telling her. For Elaine had dragged the truth out of her somehow. Women like her are fitted with radar.

Elizabeth told me afterwards that what made her most ashamed was that while Elaine was having sex with her from behind, and fingering her clitoris firmly with her left hand, she climaxed. That gave Elaine a lot of satisfaction. 'To treat me so harshly and yet extract an orgasm from me pleased her a lot.'

'It will have to last her though,' she observed with unconcealed relish. Elaine had gone too far for once. But it is an ill wind that blows no one any good. I had found the love of my life.

I met her in the park that afternoon and we drove home with the one suitcase she had managed to smuggle out.

Upstairs in the bathroom I examined her body. None of the weals had broken the skin, but they must have been very painful, just the same. I dabbed them with calomine lotion I normally kept for sunburn. John was very fond of sunbathing and usually came back looking like a lobster, so I always kept some.

Happily, John liked my new girlfriend from the start. It would have broken my heart if he had found her an incompatible personality. I told him the whole story and he was very good about it. He let me sleep with her every night for the first few weeks, with me coming in to our bed bringing the early morning tea, for the sex I never denied him.

Elizabeth, I just cuddled. I used to give her two minute non-stop kisses, but I never touched her sexually until she felt quite secure, and her whip marks had almost disappeared. Then I did. I made love to her in a way she had never known before, quietly, gently and lovingly.

My new girlfriend did everything for me and strove so hard to please me that it sometimes hurt. But, after a while, I sensed there was something missing. I had to find a substitute for the whippings. I had already noticed that if I ordered Elizabeth around a bit she climaxed more deeply in bed the next night. She was a little masochist and nothing would ever change her. If Elaine had just thrashed her with a feather duster or something, I think she would have stayed with her for ever. But I was not going to beat my Elizabeth. Neither dildos nor whips have ever appealed to me. I shall never use them of my own volition.

That evening I had a bath and changed my underclothes. Then, after dinner, I cuddled my girlfriend on the sofa all evening. We did not pet, of course, just cuddled, and I kissed her twice very deeply.

When John and I went up to bed, I carefully removed my pants and turned them inside out. They were soaked. Then I got into bed and he made love to me. I was all ready for him, but I confess I thought of Elizabeth in the next room, all the time.

After we had finished, John, like most men do, turned on his side and went to sleep. After a while I got out of bed and picked up my folded pants. The crutch was now dry and as stiff as if it had been starched. Which it had been, in a manner of speaking.

They smelt very strongly of me. Although they were clean on that evening, they had been worn for four hours by a woman on heat.

Elizabeth still had the light on and was reading. I took off my dressing gown and nightie, and slipped in beside her, putting the pants under the pillow. She turned and smiled at me sweetly.

We made love for nearly half an hour and I was on top, between her legs, with my clitoris on hers. Then I moved to the side and put my hand on Elizabeth's vagina, the fingers inside her and my thumb on her clitoris. Reaching under the pillow I said:

'Elizabeth, under your pillow I have put my soiled pants. I want you to wash the crutch as a punishment for having that last orgasm with Elaine when we were already in love.'

At the second I said that, she opened up. I could feel her heat and wetness on my hand. Nothing I had ever done or said to her had excited Elizabeth as that abrupt order did. She was trembling with suppressed excitement.

I put the pants, crutch downwards, over the girl's nose and, with an insistent intonation to my voice, told her not to touch it, merely to breath in and out.

'When I tell you, and not before, you can touch it with your tongue.' For nearly a minute I made her savour the very personal scent of the dominant female, for that is what I was, and she knew it.

Elizabeth's vagina was so wet and open I could

get my whole hand in and I took full advantage of my ability to do so. I put my fist in her, loving her dearly as I did it. And without hurting her.

'Now touch it with your tongue.' Obediently she complied.

Then I ordered her, using the same tone of voice, to put the stiff, soiled crutch in her mouth and wash it clean, so I could hang it straight on the line to dry.

Without hesitation, she did as she was told, putting her arm round my shoulders to show how willing she was. Her whole body was vibrating with submission and consent.

When I took them out of her mouth, they were clean as the day they were new, and Elizabeth climaxed on my hand, not once, but twice in succession.

Then she said, 'Next time Jane, I'll wash them for you when they are wet, the moment you take them off.' At that she wriggled down in the bed and put her head between my legs, and I was wet by then, to taste the real thing, as she said afterwards. This time it was my turn to climax and I wrapped her long, brown hair round my hand to hold her in position until I had finished. Elizabeth dried me first with her tongue and then with her now loosened hair.

I went to sleep that night with the faint smell of Jane on my girlfriend's hair. I was in heaven with Elizabeth. For the first time in my life I was in love with a girl, something I thought would never happen. And I loved her passionately.

I did as she asked the next night. My pants were

soaked, because I had kissed Elizabeth for half an hour first, and I had worn them all day this time. She washed them clean with her arm round my neck, and climaxed on my hand, even before she had finished the task.

I had at last found a way of exciting Elizabeth's latent masochism without beating her. Masochism is a perfectly normal female emotion, unless taken to extremes. Then it becomes a perversion.

I had other ways too. I found if I gave her hard work to do, found fault with it, and made her do it again, it excited her sexually. She likes me to dominate her prior to a sex session.

Occasionlly, in bed, I hold her legs wide apart at the ankles, just as she is coming up to an orgasm under my tongue. This means she has to finger her own clitoris to bring herself off.

Elizabeth is a delicate and sensitive girl, and to have to masturbate herself in front of the very eyes of the woman she loves, humiliates her. It is another version of the very deep sexual feeling she got when being whipped by a woman. In both cases she has a richer climax in consequence. But I will never beat her, I can excite her more easily and less dangerously in more subtle ways.

I love Elizabeth, but sometimes when I see her come down to breakfast looking like a candidate for the ordination of women in the English church, I just close my eyes for a second and remember her as she was only a few hours ago with her legs held wide open and handling herself so indelicately in my presence.

But on other occasions, I let her climax as she

also likes to do it, in my mouth, with her thighs pressed so tightly together I can barely breathe. That is the way we usually make love, the other is for special occasions as a variation on the theme.

John and Elizabeth and I live happily together. Lesbianism is not a well of loneliness, as one author once had it. It can be very comforting, and we conduct ourselves so that none of our present friends would guess at our relationship. They probably think she is an extra source of fun for John, though nothing could be further from the truth. She is a very good cook, so perhaps they think we keep her for the cuisine.

John says that I have discovered a lesbian extension of the maternal instinct, and that I have found in Elizabeth what Queen Anne sought in Sarah, first Duchess of Marlborough, and consummated in her passion for Abigail, Sarah's cousin. It seems it has all happened before, and in high places.

Anyway, I love my girl, and I tell my husband everything.